Dear Brio Girl,

A trustworthy friend always keeps a secret, right? Well, probably. Maybe. Maybe not. Depends.

ARE there times when secrets should be shared? Trust broken? Friendship put on the line?

Whew! Those are tough issues to battle, and if you can relate to the struggle, you'll relate to Becca as she's asked to keep secrets about the new group she's spending time with.

Hey, let us know what you think after you've finished the book. We're confident you're gonna love it. But if you don't . . . we'll refund your money, do your homework for a year, and give you a $500 shopping spree. Okay, not really. But you ARE gonna like it!

Your Friend,

Susie Shellenberger, BRIO Editor
www.briomag.com

Brio Girls®

from Focus on the Family®
and
Tyndale House Publishers, Inc.

---

1. *Stuck in the Sky*
2. *Fast Forward to Normal*
3. *Opportunity Knocks Twice*
4. *Double Exposure*
5. *Good-bye to All That*
6. *Grasping at Moonbeams*
7. *Croutons for Breakfast*
8. *No Lifeguard on Duty*
9. *Dragonfly on My Shoulder*
10. *Going Crazy Till Wednesday*
11. *When Stars Fall*
12. *Bad Girl Days*

Grasping at Moonbeams

Created by

LISSA HALLS JOHNSON

WRITTEN BY JANE VOGEL

TYNDALE

Tyndale House Publishers, inc.
Wheaton, Illinois

Grasping at Moonbeams

A Focus on the Family book published by
Tyndale House Publishers, Inc., Wheaton, Illinois 60189; First printing, 2005
Previously published by Bethany House under the same ISBN.

Cover design by Lookout Design Group, Inc.
Editor: Lissa Halls Johnson

Library of Congress Cataloging-in-Publication Data

Vogel, Jane.
Grasping at moonbeams / created by Lissa Halls Johnson ; written by Jane Vogel.
p. cm. — (Brio girls)
Summary: Sixteen-year-old Becca tries to connect her friend Solana with Christ by taking her to a new spiritual group, but she is surprised and confused when she discovers that its members are practicing Wicca.
ISBN 1-58997-052-7
[1. Witchcraft—Fiction. 2. Christian life—Fiction.] I. Johnson, Lissa Halls, 1955- II. Title. III. Series.
PZ7.V8672 Gr 2002
[Fic]—dc21 2002005578

Printed in the United States of America

11 10 09 08 07 06 05
9 8 7 6 5 4 3 2 1

For Katie N.
With apologies for borrowing her name.

JANE VOGEL has been active in youth ministry for nearly twenty years as a writer and youth worker. She is the author of several books and a contributor to several study Bibles. Jane received her MCE from Calvin Theological Seminary.

chapter 1

"How much farther, Becca?" Solana gasped. She stopped and clutched her side. Bending over to catch her breath, she leaned on her gnarled hiking stick for support.

"Shouldn't be too far," Becca answered cheerfully, not at all out of breath. She pulled a battered map out of the pocket of her cargo jeans and unfolded it. Dropping her hiking stick, she used both hands to smooth out the creases in the paper. "Look," she said, pointing to a symbol on the map. "The cliff dwellings are along this ridge, just to the—" She stopped to peer at the compass rose in the map legend. "Don't tell me—I'll get it," she said, turning the paper to line up the creek on the map with the actual creek alongside the trail. "Just to the north of Fountain Creek."

Solana shook her head. "Why I trust you with the map . . ." she began, but Becca interrupted.

"We passed this sharp bend in the creek about five minutes ago, so I figure we're right about . . . here!" she said as she made a triumphant stab at the map.

"Unh," grunted Solana, dropping to a rock and taking a swig from her water bottle. "Why does it look so close on the map and feel so far away in my legs?"

"You're out of shape, that's why," teased Becca. "That's what you get for spending the last two months doing nothing but your science project and—" she stopped abruptly. "And stuff," she finished lamely.

"And fooling around with Ramón," Solana said dryly. "Right?"

Becca squeezed her eyes shut and pressed a fist against her mouth. "Sorry!" she said. "I'm a dope for bringing it up. I wasn't thinking."

"Well, there's a surprise! Becca talking before she thinks!" Solana said sarcastically. But then her voice softened. She reached up and touched Becca gently on the arm. "Don't worry about it, *amiga*. I can learn from my mistakes." She pulled herself to her feet. "And one thing I've learned is not to let men get in the way of science! Onward to the cliff dwellings!"

"Tell me again—why did you want to test the acidity here?" Becca said as she crammed the map into her pocket and picked up her sturdy hiking stick. She was eager to get Solana's mind off her ex-boyfriend, and she knew that science was the one subject guaranteed to make her best friend forget her problems.

"I have this theory," Solana explained, "that the Anasazi who lived here centuries ago understood more about ecology than most people give them credit for. You know I did my science fair project on soil acidity. Now I want to see if I can learn anything about the acidity around the ancient cliff dwellings that might have influenced the tribes to settle there. If my theory is right . . ."

Becca smiled to herself. Solana was off and rambling about her favorite subject. Becca only half listened, knowing that soon Solana would launch into some technical aspect that would go beyond Becca's understanding, let alone her interest level. *It's good to be together like this again*, Becca thought, letting her mind wander as Solana expounded on her theory. *I was so scared that Solana was pulling away for good when she got involved with Ramón.*

Solana had been Becca's best friend since fourth grade, and Becca couldn't imagine life without her. Together with their close friends, Jacie and Tyler, they'd gone from discovering secret hideouts to discovering the opposite sex, but the one thing that never seemed to change was their friendship. "We'll make a pact," they had agreed together in eighth grade. All of them. They would be friends forever. Trusting each other to want the best for the other. Encouraging each other to grow in their relationship with God. Well, Solana agreed to encourage her friends . . . but didn't agree with the part about God.

Even when Solana insisted she didn't share her friends' faith, they'd managed to stay close. *But it's getting harder as we get older,* Becca admitted to herself. *The more we make our own decisions—about boys, or priorities, or our futures—the more it shows that Solana has different values than the rest of us. It would be easy to drift apart. We almost did over Ramón. It was as if he became Solana's whole world, and the rest of us didn't matter anymore.*

"I missed you, Sol," Becca suddenly blurted out, interrupting an enthusiastic explanation of Anasazi agriculture.

Anyone else might have been confused by the outburst, but Solana knew Becca too well. "Me too," she said with an understanding smile. "Even if you don't listen to a word I say," she added more tartly.

"I was listening," Becca protested. "Sort of."

"I can't believe you didn't have your head in the clouds instead—thinking about paragliding," Solana teased. "Or Nate," she said with a lift of the eyebrows.

"Speaking of clouds," Becca said hastily, "what kind are those?" she asked, waving her arm over her head. She wanted to avoid the subject of boys.

Solana glanced up at the puffy clouds. "Cumulonimbus, as you know perfectly well. You've only told me about 47 times that cumulus clouds show the best conditions for paragliding. Don't try to change the subject. Will Nate be there tonight?"

Becca grinned. It didn't look as if she could sidetrack Solana this time. "Oh, he'll probably stop by with Tyler," she said with a casualness that she knew didn't fool Solana. "That's *if* we get back from this hike in time," she added.

The "Brio girls," as Becca, Solana, and Jacie called themselves, usually got together on Friday nights at Becca's house. Most weekends Tyler joined them, usually with some of his guy friends. This year Hannah Connor had become part of the group too. Sometimes Hannah's parents planned "Family Night" on Friday nights, so she didn't always make the get-togethers. But Nate had been coming every weekend since Homecoming—first as Tyler's friend, but now as Becca's friend.

"Why you two want to spend all your time with the group instead of going on real dates is beyond me," Solana said.

"We do go out sometimes—you know that. But I like being in a group," Becca said simply. "I don't want to get serious—not at sixteen."

"Seventeen next month," Solana reminded her. "And lots of juniors get serious. It's not like you're freshmen."

"I like being in a group," Becca repeated. "We have fun. Besides . . ." She shot a quick sideways look at Solana, trying to decide how much she wanted to say. "Nate's really good-looking, you know?"

"Sure, if you like 'em tall, dark, and handsome. I don't anymore. Your point?"

Becca paused. Ramón had been tall, dark, and handsome, too. She didn't seem to be doing too well at keeping Solana's mind off him. *Oh, well*, she thought. *If I can't talk about Nate with Solana, then something's really wrong with our friendship*. "Sometimes I get this roller-coaster feeling in my stomach just standing next to him," Becca admitted.

"This is supposed to be news? I could have told you that six months ago!"

"And when he holds my hand, it's like grabbing an electric fence."

"Very romantic," Solana said, rolling her eyes. "Don't try writing poetry, okay? I can just hear it: *How do I love thee? Let me count the ways. Thou art more electrifying than a cattle prod, thy fingernails sharper than a barbed wire fence.*"

"Okay, so it was a bad example. All I'm saying is that being with Nate is nothing like being with Tyler—"

"I should hope not!" Solana sounded scandalized. "Tyler is practically a brother!"

"And Nate is definitely not," Becca agreed. "So I want to be smart. I mean, if holding hands and kissing feels so good—"

"Like an electric fence," put in Solana.

"Well, there's definitely some kind of electricity going on,"

Becca retorted. "And if it feels so good, I'm afraid if we're alone too much we'll want more. You know what I mean?"

"Yeah," said Solana bitterly, "I know what you mean." She forced a smile, and Becca knew she was thinking of Ramón again. "I guess you *are* smart to go slow."

Half an hour later, the girls rounded a bend in the trail and found themselves at the foot of the cliff dwellings.

"Awesome!" Solana breathed, craning her neck to peer at the ancient ruins. "Did you know that the Native Americans considered this whole area a sacred place? Not only up here, but down where the town of Crystal Springs is, too." She shivered. "It gives me goose bumps just to think of it."

Becca shivered too. "I don't know," she said, shifting her gaze from the ruins to the darkening sky above, "but maybe those goose bumps have something to do with this cold wind and those dark clouds. I bet a storm is coming over the mountains. Think we better head for home?"

"Mm-hmm," murmured Solana, slinging off her backpack and taking out a notebook and pencil. "Just let me make a few notes on the orientation of the cliff dwelling. I need to get a soil sample from here. Then I want to see if I can find any signs of agriculture and get some samples from those areas."

She began scribbling in her notebook, while Becca watched the clouds overhead. They were definitely thunderclouds. And the sky was definitely darker than it had been a few minutes ago—almost black right above them. The wind seemed to be picking up, too. Becca had lived her whole life in Colorado, so she knew how quickly the weather could turn stormy in the mountains.

"Solana!" Becca's voice was insistent now. "Those aren't

cumulonimbus clouds anymore—they're storm clouds. Let's get out of here."

"Okay," agreed Solana with a glazed look in her eye that told Becca she wasn't listening but instead was concentrating on solving some inner calculations. "The Anasazi usually built their dwellings facing south or southwest, so I would expect to find some evidence of agriculture along the base of the cliff over here, where it would get good sun." Looking at the ground, she moved slowly toward the cliff, scuffing her hiking boot in the dirt to clear off loose stones.

"Solana!" Becca repeated, grabbing her friend's arm and shaking it. "I'm serious! It's already starting to rain. We don't want to get caught in a flash flood!"

Solana blinked, as if to clear her thoughts of Anasazi agriculture, and looked at Becca. "Don't be paranoid. I studied flooding last year as part of an independent study. I can tell you the warning signs." Suddenly Solana's eyes opened wide. "Omigosh! A flash flood? Those can come up without *any* warning! Especially in the spring because of the snowmelt."

"And this *is* April," Becca said, taking the notebook from Solana's hand and unceremoniously shoving it into her backpack. "So . . . let's go!"

She grabbed Solana's arm again and pulled her back to the trail. As the girls hurried down the steep path, the rain began to pelt furiously. Within minutes Becca was drenched to the skin, even though she was wearing a thick sweatshirt and a windbreaker over her T-shirt. Only half an hour ago, the exertion of the hike had made her ready to peel off some of the layers in the warm spring sun, but now she was shivering. She looked over her shoulder at Solana, who followed her. Solana looked as miserable as Becca felt.

The rain was coming down so hard now that it was difficult for Becca to see. She tilted her head to keep the rain from streaming down her face, but then it ran down her neck inside her windbreaker. Her thick ponytail felt like a dead animal lying against her neck. She held her head straighter, but then the water dripped from her eyebrows onto her face. *I wish I had windshield wipers*, she thought. *Or even just a windshield!*

She pictured herself as an SUV, careening down the rocky trail with wipers clacking back and forth at full speed, and the mental image cheered her up a little. *This is nothing to lose my sense of humor over*, she told herself. *Gotta stay positive. Make it fun*. Taking a deep breath, she starting belting out, "I'm singin' in the rain! Just singin' in the rain!" Tyler was an old movie buff, and he'd brought a video of the musical to Becca's house one Friday night a few weeks back and forced the friends to sit through it. They all teased Tyler about how corny Gene Kelly and Debbie Reynolds were, dancing and singing under their umbrellas, but secretly Becca had actually enjoyed watching the romance blossom as the story unfolded.

"What a glorious feeling, I'm drowning again," Solana bellowed from behind her, and Becca laughed. As long as she and Solana were together, they could handle just about anything. *This will make a great story to tell the gang when we get home tonight*, she decided.

They got to the end of "Singin' in the Rain" and Becca racked her brain for another cheery song. She settled on an old favorite from her Vacation Bible School days. "The Lord said to Noah, there's gonna be a floody, floody," she began, but Solana shouted her down.

"Becca, ix-nay on the ood-flay!"

Becca turned. She hadn't heard Solana use pig Latin for years; usually Solana liked more sophisticated humor. Peering through the downpour, she realized that Solana's face looked pinched and strained. *Solana is really worried!* she realized. *She's scared!*

Solana pointed to Fountain Creek. Becca had been so busy singing, she hadn't paid attention to how the creek had changed. On their way up, the stream had run peacefully alongside the trail, but now it was rushing like water from a fire hose, splashing out of its banks and running nearly to their feet.

"Stay on the high side of the trail," Solana shouted over the roar of the stream. "When it's going this fast, even six inches of water can knock you off your feet!"

Becca nodded and turned back to continue down the trail. As she did, she stepped on a loose rock and felt it sliding out from under her. Quickly, she braced herself with her other foot, but that too skidded on the slippery trail. Grabbing a branch, she recovered her balance. *That was close!* she thought. *I could have gone right into the creek!* Shaken, she stood still for a moment, and felt Solana's hand on her shoulder as she came close behind Becca.

"How long has it been since we started hiking down?" Solana asked.

Becca pushed her sleeve up and looked at her watch—waterproof, fortunately. Then she shrugged, realizing that she didn't know what time they had left the cliff dwelling. "I don't know. Maybe fifteen minutes?"

"And how much longer till we get to town?" Solana asked.

Becca did some quick calculating. The hike from the trailhead in Crystal Springs to the cliff dwellings had taken them about an hour—an easy distance for an after-school hike. But they were going much slower now because the trail was slippery and it was hard to see. "At this rate, it could take us a couple hours," she said.

She and Solana looked at each other. Becca knew Solana was thinking the same thing she was: *In less than one hour this trail will be under water. Under very, very fast water*. She tightened her grip on the tree branch.

"Maybe we ought to—" Solana began.

"We probably better—" Becca said at the same time.

Both girls stopped. Then Solana said, "When there is danger of flood, the way to escape is to go up." The word *escape* sounded scary to Becca.

For a minute the two girls stood still as the seriousness of their situation sank in. Then Becca tossed her head, scattering water droplets like a miniature spray of wet fireworks around her. She lifted her chin. "We can do this!" she said, and set out with determination up the trail.

They trudged for a few minutes in silence. Becca knew they needed to get off the creek trail and onto higher ground, but the gorge was narrow and the walls were too steep to climb safely in the downpour. As she hiked, she tried to remember the terrain they'd covered on their way up. Did the canyon open up at all before the cliff dwellings, or would they have to go that far before they could get away from Fountain Creek? She quickened her pace as much as she dared, planting her hiking stick firmly on each step to help her maintain her balance on the slippery rock.

"Becca, wait up!" Solana called. "I can't go that fast!"

As Becca turned, a crack of lightning split the sky, followed a microsecond later by the rumble of thunder. Startled, Solana flinched, and the sudden movement made her lose her balance. Her foot slipped off the trail. The swirling waters grabbed her, sucking her into the roaring creek.

"Help me! Becca, help me!"

chapter 2

Becca flung herself toward Solana. *Oomph!* She landed on her stomach on the hard rock of the trail with a force that nearly knocked the breath out of her.

"Grab my stick, Solana," she yelled, holding her hiking stick out with her right hand while she scrabbled for a handhold with her left.

"I can't," Solana cried. "If I let go, I'll be swept away." She clutched desperately with both hands to a rock in the creek while the force of the water pulled relentlessly downstream. "Oh, Becca, help me!"

Someone help ME! Becca thought. *There's no way I can get her out by myself.* Then a flash of shame shot through her for not having thought of it sooner; *Jesus, please help me*. On hands and knees, she inched as close as she dared to the raging creek. Gripping her stick in both hands, she angled it into the water and maneuvered until the stick was under Solana's floating body, just below Solana's armpits.

"Don't let go yet," she warned. She lay down on her end of the stick, using her body weight to anchor it. "Okay," she called. "Grab it!"

The stick lurched under Becca as Solana's weight bore down on it, and for a sickening moment Becca thought it would be wrenched out of her grasp. But she held on, and slowly Solana pulled herself close enough to the bank for Becca to grab her wrists and pull her out of the water.

For a few precious moments they sat huddled together on the streaming trail. Solana was sobbing, but Becca suddenly felt calm and alert. She recognized her feelings—she'd had them before, when one of the men at the homeless shelter had surprised her in the supply room. Before she realized what was happening, he had backed her into a corner and stood, leaning toward her, his hands pressed against the wall on either side of her so she couldn't walk away. She remembered how one part of her mind seemed to be cataloging the situation with perfect detachment: noting the smell of alcohol on his breath as he leered at her and wondering how he'd made it past the check-in point when he was under the influence. She gently parried his seductive suggestions and finally talked him into leaving the storage room. It was only when she rushed into Mrs. Robeson's office to tell the director what had happened that she lost her poise and began shaking almost uncontrollably. Delayed reaction, Mrs. Robeson had called it, and she had complimented Becca for staying coolheaded in a crisis.

Well, this is a crisis if I ever saw one, Becca thought. *What would be the coolheaded way to handle it? I can fall apart later, but right now I've got to get us out of here.*

"Come on, Sol," she said, pulling Solana to her feet. "I'll hold one end of the stick and you hold the other. That way we'll be linked like mountain climbers, and if one of us slips, the other one can pull her up."

"What if the falling person pulls the other one down?" Solana asked, biting her lip.

"We won't let that happen," Becca said grimly. "We *can't* let that happen." She pressed her fist to her mouth, thinking. Then she smiled. "Come on. I have a plan."

● ● ●

"Oh, the sun'll come out tomorrow, bet your bottom dollar that tomorrow there'll be sun!" Becca warbled in her best Li'l Orphan Annie imitation. She sat on the ledge outside the alcoves that made up the cliff dwellings, her legs hanging over the edge.

"Shut up or I'll push you off," Solana grumbled, her mouth full of granola bar.

"No, really," Becca said. "The rain has stopped. I mean it."

"No, really," Solana mimicked. "This singing has got to stop. I mean it. No more musicals." She stood up and made her way over to Becca to see. "Ouch," she complained, scraping her head on the low ceiling. "Those Anasazi must have been short little dudes to make their ceilings this low." She sat down next to Becca and squinted at the sky. "Okay. So you're right. You want a medal or something?"

"No. I want an apple." Becca reached into the backpack beside her and dug through wads of junk until she located it. "I'm starving. If I'd known we were going to be here this late, I would have brought more food." She took a big bite. "Want some?" She held the apple out to Solana.

Solana shook her head and picked up Becca's cell phone instead. "If *I'd* known we were going to be here this late, I would have made sure your phone was charged before we left home," she said, looking ruefully at the "low battery" symbol flashing on and off. "My mom will never believe that I tried to call her. She'll think I was letting her worry on purpose."

"Blame it on me," Becca suggested.

"Trust me—I will," Solana shot back. "Not that it will help. Mama loves you ever since you let her teach you how to make crispy taco shells." Her voice took on a Mexican inflection as she mimicked her mother. " 'Why you don't appreciate me like that nice Becca does? Becca, she knows I am a good cook. She listens to what I have to teach her. Why can't you be like Becca?' "

Becca grinned. "She wouldn't say that if she knew that crispy taco shells and frozen pizza are the only things I can cook! Although," she added with an air of false modesty, "you could mention how clever I was to find us this shelter."

Solana looked over the edge at the trail below. "This cliff looks a lot higher from up here than it did from down there," she said. "I'm not sure if we were clever or crazy to climb it in the rain."

"It beats drowning in the creek," Becca pointed out. "And it wasn't really much of a climb, especially once we found the easy way up."

"What I don't get is how you found the easy way. I mean, I know we followed those little bitty metal prongy things, but how did you find *them* in the pouring rain?" Solana asked.

Becca put her apple down and sighed. "Solana. Those 'little bitty metal prongy things' are bolt hangers. Climbers bolt them to the rock for fixed protection on established routes."

"Huh?"

"You know—established climbing routes. Places where lots of people want to climb. You can put in permanent hardware so that everybody doesn't have to put their own pitons in every time they climb."

"Pitons," Solana repeated.

"Pitons," Becca agreed, "or bolt hangers." She looked at Solana's blank expression. "Come *on*, Solana, you must know *something* about rock climbing. Pitons and bolt hangers are what you clip your carabiners into when you're roped for a climb."

"Okay, okay. Don't get so worked up about it. What I still want to know is how you found those little bitty prongy—those bolt hangers in the pouring rain."

Becca smiled. She was secretly sort of proud of herself for noticing the bolt hangers. She took her apple and started in on it again. "You're not the only one with observation skills, you know," she said. "When you were poking around looking for signs of agriculture, I was checking out the rock face. I figured that if the Anasazi lived up *here* but farmed down *there*—" she pointed to the base of the cliff, "then there must be a pretty easy way to get up and down. I thought it might be a good place to take Alvaro for his first climb."

Solana smiled at the mention of Becca's little brother. "Kind of a long way for such a little guy to hike, isn't it?" she asked. "By the time he got here, he'd be too tired to climb."

Becca dismissed the objection with a wave of her hand. "We McKinnons are tough," she insisted. "Anyway, I was looking for an easy way up, and there was the hardware. When we came back in the rain, I just had to remember roughly where it was and follow the bolt hangers. Which is actually kind of strange," she added around a mouthful of apple, "because you don't even need to be roped on a scramble like this. We'd never have made it up in the rain if it were a route that required ropes. My guess is that beginners come here for an easy climb and to get the feel of being on a rope."

"Well, *I* used the hangers," Solana said firmly. "I held on to every one that was sticking out far enough for me to grab."

Becca rolled her eyes. "Don't tell anybody, okay? It's really bad form to hang on to your hardware instead of the rock."

"If you won't tell anybody how you had to push my big butt to get me up here, I won't tell about the hardware," Solana promised. She gave Becca a quizzical look. "How *did* you give me that boost on the butt? Didn't you have to use your hands to climb?"

Becca started to giggle. "Yeah, I was using my hands to climb, all right."

"What?" said Solana. "What's so funny?"

"When you started to sag and I gave you a boost—" Becca started, then dissolved into giggles.

"What?"

"Well, I was boosting your butt with my *head*. I climbed up right behind you and you sat down on my *head*."

"Oh." Then Solana began to giggle. "It's not that funny." But she kept giggling, until both girls were laughing hysterically.

"It's a delayed reaction to crisis," Becca explained when they finally calmed down. "Happens all the time."

"How delayed?" asked Solana. "I mean, how long have we been up here?"

Becca looked at her watch. "Only about an hour and a half," she said in surprise. "The storm didn't really last that long. We could still get to the trailhead before dark—if the trail's passable."

"The water's already going down," Solana observed, looking at the creek below them. "Want to try?"

"Sure," Becca agreed. "I don't like the thought of staying up here all night."

"Brrr! Especially in wet clothes."

"And with no bathroom."

"Becca!" Solana wailed. "Why did you say that? Now I have to go!"

"There are bushes over there," Becca suggested.

"I can wait," Solana said. "Right now all I want is to get to a working phone so I can call my mom and dad and tell them I'm okay. I bet they're worried sick."

"Yeah, mine too," said Becca. "But maybe they haven't heard about the flooding so they're not worried," she added hopefully.

But when they got to the town of Crystal Springs, there was no doubt that the flooding had made the news already.

"I can't believe it," Becca whispered. "Look."

The quaint, shop-lined main street of the little tourist town was a river of mud. Mud covered the road. Mud covered the boardwalk in front of the galleries and boutiques. Mud heaped partway up the doors and undoubtedly had found its way inside them as well.

"It looks like something out of the old *Planet of the Apes*," Becca said. "You half recognize this town poking its head out of the mud, but you can't believe it's really the town you know."

Solana stood still, moving only her head as she looked up Fountain Creek canyon, down Main Street, and across to the center of town. Her face wore what Becca called her "analyzing look."

"Mudslides," she said tersely. She caught Becca's eye. "Not just muddy water. *Mudslides*."

"Duh," Becca said. "Any dope would know that."

Solana shot her a withering glance. "We're lucky we didn't get caught in one."

"I don't think it was luck," Becca responded.

"Whatever." Solana shrugged. "The flash flood carried mud down the canyons—not just Fountain Creek, but Paxton and Cascade Creek canyons, too." She pointed to the center of town. "See how Cascade Creek runs along Main Street? It must have overflowed its banks and dropped all that mud. The worst is by the mineral springs in the center of town, because that's the lowest point." She nodded her head. "It's just like I read about in my independent study."

"What do you think happened to the people?" Becca asked in a hushed voice.

"If they were smart, they evacuated to higher ground, just like we did," Solana answered. "Look." She pointed up the hillside. "They probably went to the high school. There's no flood damage there—only in the low spots and along the creeks in the canyons." She shuddered. "Where we were."

"But if they didn't get out in time . . ." Becca's voice trailed off.

"If they didn't get out in time," Solana said in a brisk tone that didn't quite succeed in covering her emotion, "they probably ended up like that car." She pointed.

Smashed up against the concrete embankment of the bridge over Cascade Creek was a blue car. It lay at an odd angle—back wheels totally submerged in mud, but the mangled front end protruding crazily in the air. The roof looked as if it had been peeled sideways with a can opener, and all the windows were broken out.

“We could have been in serious trouble,” Becca said soberly. “I didn’t realize how serious until I saw this.” She motioned to indicate the damage all around them.

Solana turned to Becca, her dark eyes wide. The analyzing look was gone, replaced by an expression Becca couldn’t quite read. “Becca, we could have . . . I could have . . .” Solana swallowed hard.

“I know,” Becca said, grasping Solana’s arm in a quick, firm squeeze. “God really took care of us.”

“Oh, yeah?” Solana’s voice was suddenly harsh. “Then why didn’t He bother to take care of the people here? Get real, Becca. How can you look at this kind of destruction and tell me about a God who cares?”

Becca shook her head. “I don’t know,” she said honestly. “I just know that I asked Jesus to help me get you out of the creek, and He did.”

“I didn’t see any Jesus pulling me out,” Solana challenged. “That was your quick thinking and strong arms that saved me.”

“Yeah, because Jesus was helping me,” Becca insisted. “I prayed, and He gave me what it took to think fast and hold on tight.”

Solana raised her eyebrows skeptically. “Sounds like adrenaline to me. Why should you think praying had anything to do with it?”

“Because,” Becca started, then stopped. Why *did* she think God had heard and helped her? *Because I believe God answers prayer*, she told herself. *But why? I probably couldn’t give Solana any reasons that she couldn’t explain away with natural causes*. Her gaze traveled over the flooded town again. *And Solana’s right: It’s hard to see a loving God in this mess*. Suddenly she felt terribly tired. All she wanted was to get warm and dry and get something to eat.

Aloud she said, "I don't know, Sol. I'm too tired to argue about it. Let's go home." She caught her breath, her eyes wide. "Solana! What about *my* car?"

● ● ●

As it turned out, Becca's car—actually her mother's car, borrowed for the afternoon—was okay. Apparently the parking lot at the trailhead was on high enough ground and far enough from the creek that the water and mud didn't reach it.

Getting home took a lot longer than the girls had counted on, though. The only good thing about the seemingly endless detours was that they got to see people coming out into the streets to survey the damage. Becca's heart went out to the shop owners and home owners who had such a huge cleanup job ahead of them, but at least they were alive! All of the police officers they encountered on their way out of the little town assured them that, as far as they knew, no lives had been lost.

By the time Becca got home after dropping Solana off, it was late. So she was surprised to find Jacie, Tyler, Nate, and Hannah all at her house, waiting anxiously with her family. *Of course!* she realized. *I asked them all to come over at seven o'clock for a video. They would be worried and wouldn't go home once they realized Solana and I were caught in the flood!*

She took a quick shower—mercifully warm—and pulled on sweats, then went downstairs to eat the lasagna her mom had kept hot for her in the oven. While she ate, her family and friends crowded around the kitchen table and peppered her with questions. She told the story in seemingly endless detail, and by the time her friends went home she was so tired she fell into bed without even changing into her pajamas.

The last thing she remembered was her mother tiptoeing in to smooth her hair and kiss her cheek. Becca couldn't remember the last time she'd done that—not since Becca was small.

"Love you," her mother whispered.

"Love you," she murmured sleepily in response.

"You just sleep in tomorrow, Honey," her mom said. "I'll call Mrs. Robeson and tell her you won't be coming in to the community center."

Becca roused herself enough to answer. "No," she barely whispered. "Wake me up. I want to go."

chapter 

Pound pound pound.

Pound pound pound.

Becca pulled the pillow over her head. Something was making a terrible racket.

Pound pound pound.

"Becca! Are you in there?"

"Go away."

Pound pound pound.

"Becca, you'll be late for the center."

Becca jumped up to open her bedroom door. Kassy, her 12-year-old sister, stood in the hall with her fist arrested in the act of hammering on the door.

"What are you—deaf?" she said. "I must've knocked 20 jillion times already."

"Hey, I had a hard day yesterday, okay?" Becca said. "So I'm a little tired."

Kassy rolled her eyes. "If it were me, I'd be sleeping in. I don't see why you want to get up just to go volunteer at the community center. I mean, get a life."

"The center *is* my life," Becca said. "Well—the center and basketball. And volleyball. And paragliding . . . skiing . . . mountain biking . . ."

"And Nate?" Kassy asked slyly.

"No guy is ever going to *be* my life," Becca shot back. "At least not for a long time," she qualified. Then she grinned. "But Nate definitely makes life a little more interesting!"

"My *friends* are my life," Kassy said with a toss of her head that somehow made her look older than 12.

"Mine too, really," Becca agreed. "The Brio girls and Tyler. And Jesus." She paused, a little embarrassed that she hadn't thought to mention Jesus first.

"Yeah, yeah," Kassy said. "I know. Me, too." She sauntered into Becca's room and plopped down on the edge of the bed, then looked at Becca intently. "But about the Brio girls—when are you going to start taking me to the *Brio* magazine photo shoots?"

Becca looked at Kassy in surprise. "I didn't know you wanted to go. What would you do there?"

"Becca!" Kassy cried in exasperation. "What would I *do?* Be a model, of course." And she gave that unsettlingly grown-up toss of her head again.

Becca widened her eyes as she looked at Kassy speculatively. Come to think of it, Kassy was only a little younger than Becca and her friends had been when they started serving as amateur models for *Brio* magazine. It hadn't seemed like a big deal to

Becca—it was just something to do with her friends and a way to help out Tyler's mother, who worked for the magazine. Becca, Jacie, and Solana all read *Brio* magazine anyway, so when they started showing up on the pages of the magazine, the name "Brio girls" just seemed to stick. And Tyler—well, he was such a good friend from way back that he was a sort of honorary Brio girl. Since then the group had grown to include Hannah Connor, and lately Nate had been hanging around a lot . . .

"Well?" Kassy persisted. "Can I go with you to the next shoot?"

"I . . . sure, I guess," Becca said. "It's up to Tyler's mom. I'll tell her you're interested."

"Great," said Kassy, with an emphatic nod. "Now let's go."

"Go? To a *Brio* shoot? Now?" Becca was bewildered.

"No, basketball brain—to breakfast. It's newspaper time," Kassy replied.

Becca looked at her blankly.

"Honestly, Becca, didn't you hear *anything* I said when I was knocking on your door?" Kassy gave an exaggerated sigh. "I *told* you—we haven't done newspaper prayer in an age, so we're going to do it over breakfast this morning. Let's go."

Becca grabbed a robe and pulled it over her sweats before following Kassy down the stairs and into the kitchen. Their dad was already sitting at the big, battered, round oak table, drinking coffee and reading the comics from the morning paper to seven-year-old Alvaro. Alvaro, wearing his favorite Superman pajamas with a red cape, alternated between pointing at the comic strips and shoveling Cheerios into his mouth. As Becca came through the door, he must have just caught on to a punch line, because he laughed joyously and loudly, a little shower of cereal falling from his mouth.

"You're just in time, girls," Mrs. McKinnon said. "The last batch of waffles is ready. Do you want juice or milk this morning?"

"I'd like coffee, please," Kassy said, with a studied casualness that didn't fool Becca for a minute.

"Coffee?" Mr. McKinnon repeated. "When did you start liking coffee?"

"Well, I haven't actually learned to like it yet," Kassy admitted, "but I want to be ready when I start going to coffee bars."

"I don't think you'll be doing that anytime soon, Sweetie," Mrs. McKinnon said with a smile as she set a glass of orange juice at Kassy's place.

"Becca goes to the Copperchino all the time," Kassy objected.

"And I drink hot chocolate," Becca pointed out. "You don't *have* to drink coffee at a coffee bar, you know."

"Anyway, you're a little young for coffee *and* for coffee bars," Mr. McKinnon told Kassy. "Though I guess it's not all that different from that Mountain Dew you drink."

Kassy pouted. "Mountain Dew is a kid's drink. I'm practically a teenager."

"And I'm practically starving," Becca interjected. "Can we eat?" She sat down at her place and reached out to hold hands with Alvaro and her mother while her father asked a blessing on the day. As they said "amen," her mother gave her hand a little squeeze, as she always did before letting go.

Becca looked around the table with satisfaction. If basketball was her life, then her family was . . . well, her home court. *But the players have changed over the last season*, she thought to herself. Her older brother, Matt, had gone off to college last fall. Becca loved and admired Matt, but sometimes she was a little jealous of him, too. Everything Becca was good at—sports, school, having fun—Matt was better at, and with less apparent effort. *But Matt's team never made it to state*, Becca thought with a smile. The Stony Brook High girls' basketball team made it all the way to state last month, and came close enough to the championship to give Becca and the other juniors on the team high hopes for next year.

About the time Matt moved out, Alvaro had moved in. Becca's smile faded to a grimace as she remembered how she'd resented the time her parents spent on Alvaro's foster care when he first arrived from Guatemala, and how Alvaro had nearly been adopted by another couple because of her. *I can't imagine our family without Alvaro now*, she thought with a surge of love.

Then there was Kassy. Becca studied Kassy out of the corner of her eye. There it was again—signs that Kassy was changing too. Every day it seemed she was in more of a hurry to grow up. *She* looks *grown-up, too*, Becca realized, comparing Kassy's elaborate French braids with her own hastily pulled-back ponytail. *We both have longish brown hair and brown eyes*, Becca thought, *but otherwise you'd never know we were sisters.*

She helped herself to two waffles and poured a generous dollop of maple syrup over them. Her family usually didn't eat breakfast together—on school days she and Kassy left at different times—but when they all did sit down together it was always the same thing: waffles and cereal. Cooking wasn't very high on Mrs. McKinnon's list of priorities, and Mr. McKinnon could never seem to tear himself away from the morning paper long enough to do more than pour himself a cup of coffee.

Now he folded the comics page he and Alvaro had been

looking at and handed sections of the paper to the other members of the family. "Ready for 'newspaper prayer'?" he asked.

Becca nodded. One of the things she liked about her parents was the way their faith spilled out of Sunday-morning church services and into everyday events. "Newspaper prayer" was one of her favorite ways to have family devotions. Each person found an article or a headline that concerned them, and together the family would pray about each event. When they were younger, the kids usually found pictures to pray about—like Alvaro would do today. Becca smiled as she saw him reaching for the comics again. Maybe they'd end up praying for Snoopy.

"I've found mine," Kassy called out. "Listen to this: 'School Board to Debate Metal Detectors in Schools.' " She looked up from the page. "I think they're worried about guns and stuff—hold on a minute while I read the article." Frowning, she silently skimmed the page.

"I know the one I'm looking for," Becca's mom said, quickly flipping through the city section. "We were talking about it at work yesterday. Aha!" she exclaimed. "Here it is: 'City Council Denies Zoning Permit.' That's the permit for the community center to expand the homeless shelter." She put the page down and raised her voice. "You know how overcrowded we are at the center. Why, as it is we need two shifts for each meal, and we still aren't anywhere near helping the entire homeless population, not to mention the underemployed." Half rising from her chair, she leaned forward over the table. "People think that Copper Ridge doesn't have needy people, just because we're small and most people are relatively well-off. But that's simply not true—"

"You tell 'em, Mom!" Becca cheered. She shared her mother's

passion for the community center where her mom was a part-time administrator.

Her mother blinked, looked around at her family sheepishly, and sat down. "Yes, well, I guess I don't need to convince you. But those narrow-minded council members are certainly going to take some convincing."

"And prayer is a good place to start," Becca's father said mildly.

"But not stop!" Becca's mother added under her breath.

"Alvaro's found something to give thanks for," Mr. McKinnon said as Alvaro waved a picture of a Cheerios box torn from a grocery ad insert. "And here's mine: 'Mild-mannered Mother of Four Single-handedly Unseats Entire City Council.' " He grinned mischievously at his wife.

"Tom!" Mrs. McKinnon scolded, but she was smiling too.

"Okay—really, I picked an article about reopening the old mines. It seems a company has found a new, efficient way to get the ore."

"Would that be a good thing or a bad thing, Dad?" Kassy asked.

"Well, I'm not sure. That's what I think we should pray about. There's always a potential risk to the environment with mining, but if it could be done safely and cleanly it could create a lot of new jobs." He nodded at Mrs. McKinnon. "And that could help some of the underemployed people your mother is concerned about."

Becca held up the front page of the paper. "Mine is today's headline—the Crystal Springs flood!" She pointed to the grainy newspaper photographs showing streets clogged with floating debris and cars submerged to their roofs in mud and floodwater. "Nobody was killed, it says—that's good; the cops were right about that. Oh, but listen! One family had to climb onto the roof of their house to escape the water as it came racing down the canyon. They were stranded there for two hours until a helicopter rescued them!" She examined the article again. "Most of the damage was on the main street where all those little shops and galleries are. They say owners can't get in until the health department gives the okay—maybe not for a couple of days."

Kassy leaned across the table to peer at the photos. "All that damage just from water?" she said.

"Water can be a powerful force, Kassy," her dad replied, "as your sister found out yesterday. When it comes roaring down that mountain, it can flatten anything in its way."

"Sounds a lot like the city council," Mrs. McKinnon observed wryly.

"Any power can be dangerous when it's out of control," Mr. McKinnon explained to Kassy. "But remember that the water power that flooded Crystal Springs is the same kind of power that runs the turbines to create the electricity for our whole town. It's just a matter of being able to control it."

Mrs. McKinnon glanced at her watch. "If Becca's going to get to the center in time for her volunteer shift this morning, we'd better get off this sidetrack and start praying," she said.

"That's power, too," Becca's dad said with a smile. "The power of prayer." He grinned at Becca, who made a face in return.

"That's such a cliché phrase, Dad," she protested.

"I know," he replied. "But sometime clichés are true."

I suppose, Becca thought. *But . . . is praying really going to keep the guns out of Kassy's school or clear out the floodwater from Crystal Springs or get the city council to change their mind on zoning? Or is Solana right, and all it really takes is adrenaline?* She sighed. *Some of these problems seem too big for prayer* or *adrenaline. Sometimes I think we might as well put on Alvaro's cape and wish to be Superman.*

She looked over at Alvaro. He'd been sitting quietly, turning his head to look at one person after another as they spoke, almost as if he were watching a game of Ping-Pong. He'd picked up a lot of English in the eight months since he had come to the United States, but Becca realized that his English still probably wasn't good enough for him to follow the whole conversation. Now he caught Becca's eye and seemed to take that as his cue to speak.

"Thank You Jesus God for Cheerios," he said, holding his torn ad toward the ceiling, as if to give God a better view. Then he took Becca's hand and gently squeezed it. "Also amen."

chapter 

"Man, Alvaro, you're getting heavy! Did you pedal at all, or are you just along for the ride?" Becca asked as she dismounted the bike and wheeled it into the bike rack at the edge of the Outreach Community Center parking lot.

"Vrooom!" answered Alvaro, clinging to the second set of handlebars and sticking both legs straight out on either side of the bike.

"Aha! You were coasting the whole time and letting me do all the work," Becca said. "Next time you take the front seat so I can keep an eye on you," she teased as she lifted Alvaro off the bike and helped him unbuckle his helmet. Quickly she locked the bike, then led Alvaro by the hand to the back entrance of the community center, where the homeless shelter was located.

"Good morning, Becca, Alvaro," said Mrs. Robeson with a

glance at her watch as Becca and Alvaro hurried into the dining hall. Becca puckered her face in a quick grimace of frustration. She was only two minutes late and had hoped to slip in without Mrs. Robeson, the shelter director, noticing. But Mrs. Robeson always seemed to be everywhere and see everything.

"Sorry I'm late, Mrs. R.," Becca said sincerely. Mrs. Robeson held her volunteers to the same high standards set for the paid staff, and Becca hated to let her down. "Alvaro and I biked this morning, and it took a little longer than I expected."

"Alvaro biked here?" Jacie said, coming out of the kitchen with a tray of silverware. "Isn't that an awfully long way for his little legs?" She set the tray on the table and crouched down next to Alvaro. "Are you turning into a jock like your big sister, Alvaro?"

Alvaro reached out to pull one of Jacie's corkscrew curls and watch it spring back up again. Jacie gave him a hug and sent him off with Mrs. Robeson to the day care room.

"We bought one of those third wheels and attached it to the back of my mom's bike," Becca explained over her shoulder as she headed to the kitchen to wash her hands. "It makes a regular bike into a sort of tandem—only the part you attach is made for kids, so it's smaller than a regular tandem would be."

"Is it safe?" Hannah's soft voice came from the corner of the kitchen, and Becca jumped. She hadn't noticed Hannah there, folding napkins to go on the tables. "I can't imagine my mother letting the twins ride on something like that."

"Your mother is too protective," Becca said without thinking.

"It's a parent's job to protect her children," Hannah said, the determined glint in her blue eyes belying the softness of her voice.

"But it's also a parent's job to teach the children to be independent," Becca shot back with a mischievous smile. *Here we go,*

Becca thought. She and Hannah had overcome an initial dislike for each other to arrive at a mutual respect, and they loved to challenge each other to a good-natured argument.

"When they're old enough," countered Hannah, smiling. "But first the children must be taught what's right and wrong."

"But not to think for themselves, I suppose?" Becca retorted, raising an eyebrow.

"Of course to think for themselves. But to think in a way that pleases God," Hannah said, obviously enjoying the game..

"And do you think God wouldn't be pleased with Alvaro riding a bike with me?" Becca raised her hands in mock horror.

"Of course He would be," said Hannah.

"Not pleased?" Becca said.

"Pleased," Hannah corrected.

"With not biking?"

"With biking."

The girls looked at each other for a few seconds, then burst out laughing.

Becca shook her head. "What were we talking about again?"

"Congratulations!" Jacie interrupted, walking into the kitchen and making a show of enthusiastically shaking their hands. "You two have mastered the art of getting into a fight over nothing at all."

Becca grinned at Hannah. They saw their sparring as the verbal equivalent of a game of chess, but Becca suspected that Jacie, who hated conflict of any kind, was never quite sure whether the girls were having fun or really arguing.

"Why, Jacie," Becca said with feigned innocence. "We're only practicing our debating skills."

"Of course," Hannah played along. "Until we realized we were arguing the same side."

Jacie shook her head. "You two are too much alike."

"Alike!" Becca said in amazement, while Hannah's china-blue eyes widened. "We're not alike at all!" She often felt that all of her friends were so different from one another that it was almost a surprise they were friends at all.

"Look at Hannah," she commanded. "Tall, blonde, and gorgeous. A real beauty queen, even if she does hide that beautiful long hair in a bun half the time."

Hannah blushed.

"Now look at me," Becca went on. "Not so tall—but quick," she added defensively. "Dark where Hannah's blonde, muscles where Hannah is model-thin." *And that's not even mentioning the differences in how we dress!* she added silently, comparing Hannah's conservative, calf-length skirt and button-down blouse to her own jeans and sweatshirt.

"Don't be so shallow, Becca," Jacie objected. "I'm not talking about how you look."

"I'm not finished," Becca said with a mock-stern glare. "Hannah is quiet; I'm not."

"Used to be," corrected Jacie. "Once she feels comfortable she's just as outspoken and articulate as you are."

Becca quickly searched for some way they were different. "Hannah is—no offense, Hannah—a klutz; I'm a basketball star."

"Hannah is modest . . ." suggested Jacie.

Becca brushed away the implication with a wave of her hand. "Hannah is a homebody; I love adventure."

"You're both strong-minded and stubborn and you won't back down because you're sure you're right," Jacie said, raising one eyebrow and crossing her arms across her chest.

"Don't hold back, Jacie!" Becca exclaimed. "Tell us how you really feel!"

But already Jacie had dropped her defensive posture. "And you both care about people and want to help," she said in a softer voice, running her hand down Hannah's arm as if to smooth any feathers she might have ruffled.

"So let's get these tables set so these people can eat," Becca said.

"Where are Tyler and Nate?" Hannah asked. "Are they coming today? I forgot to ask them last night."

"No, they're at an orientation for summer basketball leagues," Becca answered.

"Already? It's only April!" Jacie exclaimed.

"Yeah, but those leagues fill up early," Becca said. "The whole guys' basketball team wants to be sure to get on the same league so they can practice together this summer." She grinned. "I don't think they're very happy that the girls' team went to state when the guys' team didn't even make it past regionals!"

"And you're not letting them forget it anytime soon, either, I bet," said Jacie. "What's going to happen if next year *they* have a good season and the girls' team flops?"

"We won't," Becca said confidently. "Katie's already got a training plan together for the rest of the spring so we don't lose momentum before summer leagues start up."

"Katie Spencer?" Hannah asked. "What do you think of her?"

"She's the best junior on the team," Becca answered promptly, emphasizing her reply with a percussion beat of silverware on the table. "And she's a shoo-in for team captain next year."

"I didn't mean what do you think of her as an athlete,"

Hannah said. "I meant what do you think of her as a person. You know—her views on life and God."

Becca opened her mouth to argue that an athlete *was* a person, then caught Jacie's eye and thought better of it. "Well," she began, then stopped. Katie *had* said some unkind things about Hannah in the past, making fun of her conservative wardrobe. Becca wondered uncomfortably whether Hannah had heard about that. "Well," she began again, "Katie's really popular, and she can be a lot of fun." She shot a glance at Hannah. "Sometimes she says stuff she doesn't mean, though."

Jacie seemed to sense an undercurrent to the conversation, because she jumped in to change the subject. "I asked Solana to come today, but she turned me down again. I suppose after last night she might not be feeling up to it, anyway."

"I don't know," Becca said. "After an experience like last night, I *want* to be someplace where I can help people. It seems like a good way to show I'm grateful to be alive, you know?" She shrugged, worried that maybe she sounded overly dramatic. "I wish Solana would come here just once." After two years of Becca's urging, the rest of the Brio group had finally joined her in volunteering at the center, but Solana always found some excuse not to go. "I don't know why she won't come."

"Why should she?" Hannah asked abruptly, and then mellowed. "I mean, Solana's not a Christian. The reason I'm motivated to come every week is because I feel that's what Christ would do, but what would motivate Solana?"

"She's a compassionate person, Hannah!" Becca sprang to Solana's defense. "Non-Christians do have some good qualities, you know."

"I know." Hannah picked up a napkin off the table to refold it.

"And I know Solana has great qualities. But I wonder if that's what she's depending on to get her into heaven. And we all know that's not the way."

"I don't know that Solana even believes there *is* a heaven," Becca said soberly. "God and His plan for us seems to be the one thing Solana won't talk about."

"That doesn't make sense to me," Hannah replied. "I mean, you've known her for six years and she still doesn't even seem close to accepting the Gospel."

"Seven years," corrected Jacie. "And it doesn't make sense to us either." She shot a sideways glance at Becca. Becca knew what she was thinking. They'd talked about it often enough. Why, no matter what they said to Solana, or how they said it, or how hard and often they prayed for her, or how they tried to be attractive examples of faith, did she still remain unmoved? The only time she could ever remember that Solana seemed to soften was when they prayed for her relationship with Ramón in Alyeria. For about a week, she didn't attack anything they'd said about God. But then the walls seemed to go up again and the sassiness had returned.

Hannah began spacing the chairs around the table. "I thought last night—what if Solana had died in the flood? She would've spent eternity without Christ."

"I know, I know," said Becca, hoping the guilt wasn't showing on her face. She'd been so concerned about getting the two of them to safety, the thought of Solana's salvation hadn't even crossed her mind. "But what was I supposed to do—hold her down and baptize her while she was in the water?" She paused, then said seriously, "Honestly, I don't know what more to do besides what we've been doing."

Jacie stepped in. "You know we pray for her, Hannah. You've

prayed with us. I agree with Becca. I don't think there's anything else we *can* do. It's up to God."

"I don't get it." Hannah slumped in one of the folding chairs and gazed at something far away. "God says in His Word that it's His will that we all come to a saving knowledge of Him. And if you've been praying for her and sharing God with her for years, then it feels like God should have done something by now. 'Ask and ye shall receive.' " She mumbled the last words as if saying them only to herself.

What was Hannah getting at? The three of them had engaged in numerous conversations about Solana, and Becca always left feeling like she wasn't doing enough. "Do you think we're praying wrong?" asked Becca, with an edge in her voice.

"No, of course not!" Hannah said hastily. "Or . . . well, I don't know. But I do know God answers prayer."

She sounds so certain, Becca thought. "How many friends have you prayed for that got saved?" she asked curiously. She wasn't trying to challenge Hannah; she really wanted to know.

"Lots of people!" Hannah beamed. "Why, at last fall's evangelism conference alone, I prayed with three people who accepted Jesus. Not that it was my doing," she added quickly. "The Spirit was really working."

"Yeah, I remember," Becca said. "And that was really cool. But I wasn't thinking of strangers that you witness to. I meant, regular friends who just don't seem to care about God."

"Oh." Hannah seemed, for once, at a loss for words. "Well, no one." She looked from Becca to Jacie and hurried on. "But that's only because I've never had any non-Christian friends besides Solana."

"Well, then maybe your prayers aren't good enough either,"

Becca said with a little more attitude than she'd intended.

Hannah took in a breath, but said nothing. She clasped her hands in front of her and looked down at the ground as though trying to find the answers there.

"I wasn't trying to say your prayers aren't good enough," Hannah finally said. "I just mean that Solana's salvation is at least as important as, oh, going to an artists' conference or winning your basketball games." She looked from Jacie to Becca. "I see how much effort you put into those things—I just think you should be as serious about something with eternal consequences."

Becca opened her mouth, then shut it again. Even she couldn't find anything to argue with on that point.

chapter 5

The gondola lurched to a stop and Becca stepped out onto the platform into the Saturday afternoon sun.

"Hi!" she called to the attendant as he hefted her heavy pack of paragliding gear off the rack on the gondola roof. "How's the wind today?"

The attendant squinted at the sky, watching the half-dozen or so paragliders sailing above the ridge. "Not bad for April," he said, turning his attention back to Becca. "Not much in the way of thermals—it's still kinda cool."

Becca nodded. Thermals—updrafts of hot air that could keep a paraglider in the air for hours—developed mostly on summer afternoons, not on cool days like today. But even without thermal conditions, the way the air moved up along the mountain made enough ridge lift to give a paragliding pilot a pretty good ride. She smiled in anticipation.

The attendant smiled back and set Becca's gear on the platform. "You come here often?" he asked, cocking an eyebrow at her.

Oh, please, Becca thought, just barely managing not to roll her eyes. *Not that old line!* She looked at the attendant, who was now looking her up and down. *Probably a ski bum*, she decided, noticing how tanned his face was for April. *I bet he worked here all winter so he can ski for free*. Spring skiing usually lasted till about mid-April, but the snow had started melting early this year. Becca was glad; the Copper Ridge ski area didn't open the slopes to paragliding until ski season was over.

"I come here now and then," Becca told him. *Like every Saturday afternoon when the weather is good*, she added silently. *But you don't need to know that!*

The ski bum moved a step closer. "I'll probably be seeing you, then," he said. "I'll be working this lift all summer. My name's Danny," he added with another lift of his eyebrow.

Thinks he's God's gift to women, I'll bet, Becca thought. *He is cute*, she admitted. *And way too sure of himself!* She bent down to pick up her gear.

"Better let me help you with that," Danny said, stepping close to Becca so that his arm brushed hers. "It's pretty heavy for a cute little thing like you."

With one fluid motion, Becca swung the 30-pound pack up from the floor and onto her back, hitting Danny square in the chest on the upswing.

"Oooof," Danny gasped as the force knocked him against the platform railing.

"Oh, Danny, I'm *sooo* sorry!" Becca cooed in her most innocent voice. "I'm such a little thing, I guess I just don't know my own strength." She flashed him her sweetest smile as she walked away.

Tipping her head back, she squinted at the paragliders in the air above her. From a distance, they looked like colorful eyebrows floating in the sky. On those closer to the ground, though, she could pick out a pilot sitting in the sling under each eyebrow-shaped wing. Scanning the figures on the mountainside, Becca was pleased to spot her friend Otis, just laying out his blue-and-green wing in preparation to launch.

"Otis!" she called, waving.

Otis looked up from untangling the dozen or so lines attached to his glider. "Hey, Kid! They let you out of school early?"

"Otis, it's Saturday," Becca said before she noticed the twinkle in Otis's eye and realized he was teasing her. She looked around; as usual, she was the youngest one on the ridge. Otis, she thought, was one of the oldest of the "regulars" that came to paraglide, although she'd never asked him his age. She didn't even know his last name. *It is a funny kind of community that develops among paragliding pilots*, Becca thought. Some of them saw each other nearly every day, but nobody seemed to know much about anybody's life outside of paragliding. Otis didn't know her first name until he saw it on her dog tags once. And he still called her by the nickname he'd given her when she first started gliding last summer.

"Let me help you launch, Kid," Otis said. "With these patches of snow around, it's pretty hard to do it by yourself." He cocked an eye at the sky. "It's getting crowded up there—you be careful."

"Crowded?" Becca echoed. "There's only six flyers up there." She counted again. "Five paragliders and a hang glider."

"And four more on the ground ready to launch," Otis growled as he helped Becca pull her wing out of her pack and unroll it on the ground. Otis gave a jerk of his head toward the windsock mounted on a six-foot pole near the edge of the ridge. It fluttered slightly. "That's enough when the winds are this light."

Becca nodded.

"You need more room to navigate in light winds," Otis continued. "In a strong wind, you can stay up just about anywhere. But if the wind is light, sometimes you have to follow it to keep your wing from collapsing." He dropped the lines he'd been laying out and held up his hands about a foot apart to demonstrate. "Look: the wind starts dropping off—" he wobbled his hands as if they were paragliders losing lift, "and everybody goes to where the gusts are stronger." He moved his hands toward each other. "Pretty soon you got no elbow room up there."

"Okay—I'll keep my elbows in," Becca said. She patted him on an arm. "I know all this, Otis," she said gently. "But thanks for always teaching me." She pulled on her protective overalls and strapped on her helmet.

"Well, you just keep your eyes open for anybody moving in on your space," Otis insisted. He looked at her speculatively. "Speaking of moving in on you . . ." He stopped.

"Yeah?" Becca prompted.

"Well, it's none of my business, but I was just wondering if you met the guy who runs the gondola."

"Danny?" Becca laughed. "Yeah—I think I made a pretty big impression on him. Hit him hard in the heart, you might say."

"He's got a reputation, Kid, and I wouldn't like you to get hurt. If he asks you to watch the moon rise from the top of the mountain some night, you might want to take your wing along.

Otherwise there's no getting back down until he's ready to run the gondola. And from what I hear, that might be after he's seen more than the moon."

"Thanks, Otis. I appreciate your concern." Becca smiled. "But you know I try to live for Jesus. And that doesn't leave room for moonlight encounters with guys who try to pick me up on the gondola!"

"Okay," Otis nodded. "I don't know much about that living for Jesus stuff, but I'll take your word for it."

"I'd love to tell you more about it, Otis," Becca said. "Living for Jesus is as big a rush as any paragliding flight!"

"That's what you've been telling me," Otis said noncommittally. "If it works for you, that's great."

"It works because it's real," Becca said. "Jesus is—"

"Kid, I've got plenty of time for religion later. Right now I just want to get you airborne before Bowser over there cuts into your launch space." He nodded in the direction of a pilot unrolling a red-and-white wing. "You got all your gear on?"

"Yup," said Becca. "I've even got a cell phone. And the battery's charged." She smiled shamefacedly. "Ever since that one time I blew off course, my dad won't let me fly without some way to get in touch with civilization."

Otis chuckled. "Smart man, your dad. Just don't go making any calls while you're flying. Nothing worse than pilots who don't keep their focus on flying." He shot a look at Bowser. "Dangerous fools, some of them."

"You've just got it in for Bowser," Becca laughed.

Otis shook his head. "Gliding is a serious sport," he reminded Becca. "When you're up at 5,000 feet, you've got no business being careless and putting other pilots at risk."

"Yes, sir!" Becca saluted. "Requesting permission to launch, sir!"

Otis double-checked the clips that attached Becca's wing to her harness. "Go ahead and launch face-forward," he said. "That way you can watch out for the ice patches. I'll get your wing in the air."

Becca walked downhill until the cords to the wing were taut. For a solo launch, she would normally turn around and jerk the cords to lift the wing into the air. Then she'd have to pivot quickly to face downhill again before the cords tangled. But with Otis helping her, she didn't have to worry about turning.

"Hey, Otis," she called over her shoulder as a thought struck her. "Who's going to help you launch in this ice?"

"Don't worry about me," Otis answered. "I've done so many winter launches, I've lost count. This little bit of snow isn't gonna bother me any." He motioned for her to face forward again. "You ready? On the count of three."

Becca counted aloud with him. "One—two—three!" She felt the tug on the harness that told her the wing was aloft, and she began to lope downhill in long, easy strides, making sure not to slip on the snow. *It's just like climbing invisible steps*, she thought, as the wing lifted her off the ground and suddenly she was running in air.

Whoosh! Becca exhaled and realized she'd been holding her breath. *I wonder if you ever get over this thrill?* she thought. *Being able to fly—what could be better than that?*

She leaned back into her harness and adjusted her grip on the hand toggles. Otis was right—the wind did seem a little fickle. One minute her wing was beautifully buoyed with wind filling every one of the tube-shaped cells that made up the wing; the next minute part of the wing was deflating like a balloon two days after a birthday party. She was going to have to concentrate if she didn't want her wing to collapse completely.

For a few minutes Becca experimented with spiraling to get the maximum amount of lift. She noticed that the other pilots were following a similar pattern. *We're like jets lined up in a landing pattern above an airport*, she thought. *I bet Otis would like to have an air-traffic controller here—he's such a safety freak.*

She looked around for him. She spotted his blue-and-green wing slowly circling above the forested area on the northern end of the ridge, making the most of the updrafts the way the hawks and eagles do. Like one of those great soaring birds, Otis had been known to stay up for hours. After more than 500 flights, he knew just how to gauge the wind and control his wing so that his spirals looked effortless.

The hang glider Becca had seen earlier crossed into her field of vision and attracted her attention. If paragliders looked like eagles, a hang glider looked like some bizarre overgrown butterfly, with the pilot encased in a horizontal harness that looked just like a giant cocoon. It was fast though—faster than a paraglider. Harder to learn, too, a lot of people said.

While the paragliding pilots made slow, lazy-looking spirals to catch the best lift, the hang-gliding pilot zigzagged back and forth above the ridge like a sailboat tacking against the wind. *I bet that would drive an air-traffic controller crazy*, Becca thought. She watched as the pilot rickracked his way south along the ridge, climbing higher with every change of direction. When he reached the gondola, he reversed directions and headed north, still climbing. This time he passed directly above Becca. She looked up and saw his shadow on her wing. *How much higher is he than I am?* she wondered idly.

She watched as the hang glider traversed his way to the northern edge of the ridge. *My depth perception is off up here*, she thought. *I guess it's because there's no background to give perspective. That hang glider looks like he's practically on top of Otis.* Suddenly she leaned forward in her harness. *What does he think he's doing? He's going to fly right into Otis!*

"Otis!" Becca screamed. "Look out!"

As Becca watched, the hang glider collided with Otis with a force that Becca could almost feel. Otis's wing sagged, then collapsed completely.

"Otis! No!"

Otis plunged in a free fall toward the forest below.

chapter 6

He'll be all right. He'll be all right, Becca repeated to herself over and over, as if saying so could make it true. *Otis will be all right. He has to be all right.*

But her heart pounded wildly and she had a sick feeling in her stomach. She'd never seen a midair collision before. She didn't know for sure, but it didn't look as if there were any way Otis could have gotten his wing open to stop his fall. He had a reserve chute, of course—but had he been able to pull the cord in time to get it open? For all Becca knew, he could have been stunned from the impact of the hang glider.

"Dear Jesus," Becca said aloud, "please take care of Otis! Don't let him—" She swallowed hard before she could even say the word. "Don't let him die."

Otis's words echoed in her memory: "I've got plenty of time for religion later."

Oh, Otis, what if your time is up?

Becca peered at the wooded area that Otis had fallen into, but she couldn't see any sign to indicate where Otis had landed—or crashed. Remembering her cell phone, she thought, *I can call for help!*

The cell phone was in the storage pocket on her harness. According to the salesperson who had sold Becca her paragliding gear, the pocket was supposed to have "easy in-flight accessibility," but as Becca fumbled with the zipper she decided that claim might have been more sales hype than reality. She hadn't needed to get into the pocket while she was in the air before, and she was surprised at how awkward it was to work the zipper while still controlling her wing. She was beginning to understand why Otis warned her not to mess with her phone while she was flying. A lapse of focus for just a few moments could send her into some other paraglider the way the hang glider had crashed into Otis.

"Hold on, Otis," she called. She knew he couldn't hear her, but she felt better saying something than staying quiet. "I'm going to land, and then I'll call 9-1-1 for you right away!"

● ● ●

It seemed like hours after her phone call before Becca heard the med-evac helicopter overhead, and hours more while she watched it circling the area where Otis had gone done among the trees. Finally the helicopter dipped out of sight behind the ridge.

"Does that mean they've found him?" Becca asked the other gliders who, like her, were watching somberly from the base of the ridge. Most just shrugged. It was impossible to know what was happening down in the forested valley on the other side.

Becca pressed her fist hard against her mouth and blinked quickly to keep the tears welling up in her eyes from falling. At last the chopper rose into sight again. For a second, the noise of the rotor filled Becca's ears, then the helicopter was gone.

● ● ●

"No, I don't know his last name, but his first name is Otis. Can't you please check and see if anyone named Otis was admitted today? He would have come by helicopter."

Becca covered the receiver with her hand. "Same old story," she whispered to her dad. "They say they only track patients by their last names."

She turned back to the telephone for one last try. "Please, it's really important! He's a friend of mine—Now listen, lady!" She stopped when her father raised a warning eyebrow at her. "Okay. Thanks anyway," she muttered as she hung up the phone.

"You began to sound a little rude there, Becca," her dad said quietly.

"The switchboard operator had the nerve to say Otis must not be much of a friend if I didn't even know his last name," Becca said in frustration. "What does she know? With an attitude like hers, I bet she doesn't have *any* friends."

"She's just trying to do her job," Becca's dad said reasonably. "Was that the last hospital on the list?"

"Yes," Becca groaned, flipping the yellow pages shut. "I've called every hospital from here to Denver, and nobody can tell me anything about him. Dad, I don't know if he's hurt or . . . or if he's even alive!"

"I know, Honey," her dad said, resting his hands on Becca's

shoulders and squeezing gently. "But you've done all you can. Why don't you go to bed now?"

"Don't tell me I'll feel better in the morning, 'cause I won't," Becca threatened. Her dad just smiled and kissed her on the forehead.

• • •

SATURDAY, APRIL 7—LATE!

DEAR JOURNAL,

MY DAD SAYS I'VE "DONE ALL I CAN." BUT I HAVEN'T DONE ANYTHING! I'VE NEVER FELT SO HELPLESS IN MY WHOLE LIFE!

I SAW THAT HANG GLIDER MOVING INTO OTIS'S AIR SPACE—I SAW IT! BUT I COULDN'T DO ANYTHING ABOUT IT.

THEN I SAW OTIS FREE FALL. AND I COULDN'T DO ANYTHING ABOUT THAT EITHER.

AT LEAST I CALLED FOR HELP. THAT WAS SOMETHING. BUT I DON'T EVEN KNOW IF THE HELICOPTER GOT TO OTIS IN TIME, OR WHERE THEY TOOK HIM.

MY FAMILY THINKS I'M ASLEEP NOW. AFTER ALL, "I'VE DONE ALL I CAN."

WHAT THEY DON'T KNOW—WHAT I'M TOO ASHAMED TO TELL THEM—IS THAT I DIDN'T DO NEARLY ENOUGH.

WHAT IF TODAY WAS MY LAST CHANCE EVER TO TALK TO OTIS? WHAT IF OUR CONVERsation was the last one he ever had? And instead of telling him about how he can know Jesus, I let him go with that lame excuse about having "plenty of time."

Maybe Hannah is right about me.

No, forget that. Hannah can't be right.

But maybe she's a little right. Maybe I do need to get more serious about connecting my friends with Christ.

It might be too late for Otis.

But it's not too late for Solana.

Becca closed her journal and rolled over on her bed to gaze up at the ceiling. She let her eyes drift to her bulletin board. It was cluttered with mementos of the basketball season—news clippings, photos, and, in the very center, her ribbon from the state tournament.

Suddenly Becca got up. She pulled open the top drawer of her desk and poked through the haphazard collection of papers, old journals, and photos until she found what she was looking for: a picture of Solana. With a determined look on her face, she thumbtacked the photo in the center of her bulletin board, right over her tournament ribbon. She stepped back and looked hard at the bulletin board, then nodded.

"Solana, you're my best friend," she said to the picture. "You and Jesus. I've just got to find a way to get you two together."

chapter 7

"Hey, Becca!"

Becca set her tray next to Solana's brown bag on the table and looked up to see Katie Spencer weaving her way through the Monday lunchroom crowd.

"Change in plans," Katie said. "We're not doing our training drill after school today."

"No drills?" Tyler inquired around a mouthful of beef-and-bean burrito. "What could be more important than getting the mighty girls' basketball team ready to win next year's state championship?"

"Which is only—let me see," Solana interrupted, pretending to count on her fingers, "11 months away." She rolled her eyes at Jacie. "These jocks!"

"When I want something, I do what it takes to make it happen," Katie retorted.

Becca smiled to herself. That was one of the things she liked about Katie. And it seemed to work for Katie—she was not only a star player on the court, but she was also one of the most popular girls in the junior class.

"So what *is* more important today than training?" Becca echoed Tyler's question.

"Helping a friend," Katie answered promptly. "You know Willow Cunningham?" Becca nodded. She'd seen Willow around, although they'd never had any classes together.

"Her mom has a gallery/shop in Crystal Springs," Katie continued, "and they got flooded over the weekend. I'm going there right after school to help with the cleanup."

"Becca and I got caught in that flood," Solana said with a shiver. "I've never been so scared in my whole life. Did your friends get hurt?"

"No, they're fine," Katie said. "But everything in Crystal Springs is such a mess! It just makes me want to do something to help, you know?"

"Do I ever!" Becca said with feeling. Doing something to help was about all she'd had on her mind the entire weekend.

Jacie seemed to know what Becca was thinking. "Becca's worried about a friend too," she explained to Katie. "He was in an accident Saturday, and Becca doesn't know what happened to him." Jacie laid her hand on Becca's arm. "Becca's not so good at sitting still."

"You need any help today?" Becca asked Katie. "Since we're not practicing today, I've got time."

"That would be great," Katie said.

"Count me in," Solana said.

"Me too," Jacie chimed in. "I don't have to work today. How about you guys?" she asked the others.

"Sure," said Tyler at the same time that Nate said, "Sorry."

Nate shook his head regretfully. "Ty, we promised to get together with our study group and finish that project for English class today."

"Oh, we could do that another time," Tyler said cheerfully.

"That's what you said last week," Nate reminded him.

"Don't think you can wait till the last minute and turn in junk," Solana warned. "Mr. Garner doesn't stand for that."

"And think how disappointed he'd be in you," Jacie added.

"Okay, okay," Tyler said, throwing up his hands in mock surrender. "Nate and I will wade through *Huckleberry Finn* while you girls have fun wading in the mud."

"How long will the cleanup take?" Hannah asked in her soft, clear voice.

"I don't know—maybe till 9 or 10?" ventured Katie.

"On a school night?" Hannah seemed a little upset. "Oh, I'm sorry. I'd like to help, but my parents wouldn't want me out that late."

"I could bring you home earlier," Jacie offered. "I can't stay that late either," she said to Katie. "Too much homework."

"That's okay," Katie said. "Come for as long as you can." She told the girls how to find the gallery and they agreed to meet there after school.

"Be sure to wear boots and gloves," Katie said over her shoulder as she walked away. "It'll be a dirty job!"

When the girls pulled up to the *Earth & Stars* gallery in Jacie's little green Toyota Tercel that afternoon, Katie was sweeping water out the doorway with a push broom.

"Hi!" she called, straightening up and brushing her hair out of her face with the back of a muddy, gloved hand. "Didn't Hannah come after all?" she asked, looking from Becca to Jacie to Solana.

"No, she had some stuff she had to do at home," was all Jacie said. On the way to the gallery, Jacie told Becca that Hannah needed to do more than just "stuff." Hannah's mom had been torn. She wanted Hannah to have the chance to help, but she needed her to baby-sit the twins while she took the older ones to the dentist. Mrs. Connor often relied on Hannah to make dinner and watch the younger children several times a week. Becca had to admit she admired Hannah for her positive attitude about it all. Hannah loved being the substitute mom and homemaker—most of the time.

"Come on in and I'll show you what to do," Katie said, and the girls followed her inside.

The damage wasn't as bad as Becca had expected. While the mud along the streets had been up to several inches deep before the sanitation crews had come through, only a light coating covered the floor of the gallery.

"Looks kind of like my uncles' stables when they haven't been mucked out for a while," Solana commented.

"It reminds me of the slurry we use in ceramics class when we're making pottery," Jacie observed.

"Good call, Jacie," Solana said approvingly. "Slurry is sediment dissolved in water, and that's about what this is."

"And today's Minute for Science is brought to you courtesy of Science Geeks Unlimited," Becca intoned in her best radio announcer voice, then jumped to dodge the splash of mud Solana kicked her way.

Jacie was looking around the gallery with interest, and Becca followed her gaze, knowing that Jacie was looking with an artist's eyes. Like many of the businesses in Crystal Springs, *Earth & Stars* was part gallery, part gift shop. Native American dream catchers hung from hooks in the ceiling. Stained-glass rainbows, angels, and unicorns caught the light coming through the mud-spattered windows.

Solana wandered over to a shelf of geodes and crystals. *Probably mentally cataloging them into geological categories*, Becca thought. A shelf to her right was draped with a blue and silver cloth on which candles, oils, and incense were attractively arranged.

A door opened at the back of the gallery. Willow Cunningham, armed with a sponge mop and bucket, trailed behind a tall, thin woman who carried several brooms into the main room. Even though she was dressed to work, the woman managed to look classy, not grubby. Her black jeans were streaked with mud, but they made her long legs look even longer. Even her jagged-hemmed black shirt looked artistic rather than ragged. Long silver earrings dangled from her ears, each a little galaxy of moons and stars.

"Raven," Katie said, "this is Becca, Solana, and Jacie. They came to help." She turned to Becca and her friends. "You know Willow, right? And this is her mom."

"Hi, Mrs. Cunningham," Becca said. "Glad to meet you."

"Call me Raven," she said with a smile. "Anyone willing to help with this mess has to be a first-name friend."

"What a pretty name," Jacie exclaimed. "It's so unusual."

"Well, my parents named me Maude," Raven admitted, "but I like Raven better."

"It fits your hair," Jacie said, and Becca thought she was

right—Raven's glossy black hair, swept up in a loose knot on the top of her head, did remind her of bird wings. Becca looked curiously at Willow. She hadn't expected her to have such an exotic-looking mother. Every now and then Willow went in for what Becca thought of as the "artsy look"—black flowing clothes and jangly necklaces. But most of the time she seemed pretty ordinary.

"First step is to finish sweeping the mud and water out of this room—and I have plenty of brooms!" Raven laughed. "While you girls push this glop out the door, I'll go out and try to wash some of the grime off the windows."

Becca and the others took the brooms and set to work. It was harder than Becca had expected; the mud was thin enough that it flowed around the broom and filled in the areas she had just cleared.

"I'm surprised it's still this wet," she said to Willow, who was working beside her.

"Yeah—but it started a lot wetter!" Willow replied. "Actually, we were afraid it would dry out and cake to the floor before we got it cleared out."

"Why did you wait so long to start cleaning up?" Becca asked without thinking, then quickly pressed her fist to her mouth when she realized she might sound like she was criticizing.

"*Do it now*, that's Becca's motto," Jacie said smoothly, covering Becca's embarrassment.

"We weren't allowed in until today," Willow explained. "The building inspector had to make sure there was no structural damage. They've had a whole team of inspectors working around the clock just so people can begin cleaning up."

"Wow, you're lucky there wasn't any damage," Solana said.

“I don’t think it was luck,” Katie said, and Becca saw Solana raise her eyebrows.

“Yeah?” Solana challenged. “That’s twice I’ve heard that lately. Seems like luck to me.”

“Some people look at it that way,” Katie agreed. “I happen to believe in spiritual protection.”

“Me too!” said Becca, flashing Katie a smile. Solana didn’t quite roll her eyes, but the look she shot Katie was pretty skeptical.

“You’re a science freak, aren’t you, Solana?” Katie persisted. “So tell me this: Have you ever come through something safely when the scientific odds were against it?”

Solana was silent a moment, then muttered, “Yeah, I guess.”

“Like about 72 hours ago,” Becca said under her breath, and Solana jabbed her with her broom.

“So, scientifically speaking,” Katie went on, “is it more reasonable to say that something just happens, or that every action has a cause?”

“A cause, of course,” Solana said, “but—”

“So all I’m saying,” Katie interrupted, “is that I don’t think being protected is luck. I think something caused it.” She grinned. “Science and spirituality don’t *have* to disagree, you know.”

You tell her! Becca cheered silently. *Maybe* that’s *the way to get Solana thinking about God—by appealing to her scientific nature.*

“Hmm,” was all Solana would say, but Becca could tell she found Katie’s argument interesting.

When the floor was finally as mud-free as the girls could get it, Raven came and inspected, her hands on her hips. She gave a nod of approval.

“Good work, girls. I appreciate it. We’ll call it quits for

tonight. Tomorrow morning I'll give it a good mopping, and then I should be ready to start on the nasty task of disinfecting." She wrinkled her nose. "Health department requirements—just in case there was any sewage in the flood water."

"Lucky—I mean, good thing you have a tile floor instead of carpet," Solana said.

"Oh, there's always good to be found if you know where to look for it," Raven said with a smile. She stretched out her hands to the girls. "And you have done such a good thing for me, I'd like to give you a little token of thanks." She moved gracefully to the window and unhooked five little stained-glass rainbow suncatchers, one for each girl.

"The rainbow after the storm," said Katie, delighted. "How perfect! Thank you!"

"The sign of promise," Jacie said quietly, nestling her suncatcher in her hand.

"I think of that every time I go gliding," Becca said. "That's the brand name on my wing, you know—Promise. And of course the wing is shaped kind of like a rainbow." The smile faded from her face as she thought about Otis. *Was there a promise anywhere for him?*

Jacie picked up on Becca's mood quickly. "What's the matter, Becca?"

"Thinking about Otis," Becca said heavily.

"Who's Otis?" Katie asked.

"My friend who had the accident Saturday," Becca explained, then told Katie, Willow, and Raven the whole story.

"Wow, I'm sorry," Katie said. She hesitated, as if deciding whether to say more. "Would you—" she shot a look at Raven that Becca didn't quite understand. "We could pray for Otis this week. Would that be okay?"

"That would be great," Becca said sincerely. "Thanks, Katie."

● ● ●

On the way home, Solana was quieter than usual. Jacie, too, seemed lost in her own thoughts. Finally Becca leaned forward from the backseat to break the silence.

"It felt good to help out, didn't it?"

"Uh-huh," Solana agreed. "I'm glad we went. Especially since we were there during the flood. It feels right to do something to help . . ." Her voice trailed off.

"What felt right to you, Solana?" Jacie asked. "Did you feel—" Jacie left the sentence hanging.

"I don't know. I guess I enjoyed Katie Spencer more than I expected, for one thing," Solana answered. "I always thought she was kind of shallow, but she said some pretty interesting things today." She turned to Becca. "Does she talk about spiritual stuff like that all the time?"

"No, not really." Becca thought for a moment. "I think she's mentioned praying a couple times, but that's about all. She's never shared anything much about her faith with the basketball team. I don't know why."

"Maybe she feels it's too private," suggested Jacie.

"Or maybe she doesn't get a chance, the way Becca is always talking about God," Solana said, with a teasing note in her voice.

"I wish I could do that," Jacie started, but Becca and Solana cut her off.

"Not again!" Solana cried.

"Jacie, quit it!" Becca said. "Quit comparing your way of

sharing your faith with my way. Everybody's different."

"Raven is sure different," Solana said with a chuckle. "Can you imagine any of our mothers looking like that when they're working around the house?"

Becca started to giggle as she pictured each of their mothers in turn.

Solana's mom—round and comfortable and homey. When you looked at her, you'd always think, "Good food," not "Gallery owner." And Jacie's mom . . . Becca realized with a stab of sympathy that Jacie's mom always seemed so tired, so focused on making ends meet, that anything else seemed almost frivolous.

Then there was her own mom—tailored and super-practical. But when she put on her Saturday morning grubbies—jeans and an old flannel shirt that belonged to Becca's dad—she certainly didn't have the aura of glamour that Raven had. Even so, she wouldn't bat an eye at Raven's appearance. That was one thing Becca loved about her mom: She seemed to look right past externals.

"Raven's not your typical mother, that's for sure," Becca said. "But I liked her."

"You did?" Jacie asked.

"Well, sure," Becca said, surprised at the question. "Didn't you?"

"I don't know," said Jacie hesitantly. "Maybe it wasn't Raven so much as the gallery. I just didn't feel good about it, somehow."

"Too touristy," pronounced Solana. "That's why you didn't like it. You're an artist, and no real artist likes anything that makes money. You'd rather starve in a garret—whatever that is," she added. "I always meant to look it up so I could know where all these artists are starving."

"Don't bother—Jacie's not going to be a starving artist. She's going to be a wildly successful one," Becca said. She felt a warm glow inside, like an ember radiating in the center of a fireplace. In the face of all the things that were out of her control—the flood, Otis's accident—today she'd found a way to help someone else. Katie was going to pray for Otis. And just maybe Solana was getting curious about spiritual things.

chapter 8

"You don't want to go?" Becca stared blankly at Solana.

"Bright girl. You figured out what *no* means." Solana sighed in exasperation.

"But you said yes before—"

"ONCE! I said yes once." Solana shook her head and said softly to herself, "I *knew* I should never have said I'd go."

"So you could say yes again," Becca said firmly.

"I only said yes because I'd reached a low point in losing Ramón. I didn't want to be alone. There was no speaker. It was just playing all night with my friends at Crazy Charlie's Fun Center. Emphasis on fun. Not church; not God. Fun. And once does not make a pattern. I'm sorry if my going ever made you think I'd go again."

Becca opened her mouth to speak, then shut it again. *But you seemed willing to listen to spiritual ideas when we were talking with Katie*, she wanted to say. *And I made a commitment to get serious about connecting you with Christ. I put your picture in the center of my bulletin board.*

Once a month, all the area youth groups got together to sponsor a Friday night event called The Edge. Packed with high-energy competitions and music and concluding with a low-key speaker who talked about faith in a way anyone could understand, The Edge gave the Christian kids from area high schools a chance to spend time with each other, but it was also a nonthreatening place to invite their non-Christian friends. Becca and the rest of the Brio friends went every month, and Becca always had a blast. But Solana persistently refused their invitations.

"Becca, you know I don't do church things," Solana said.

"But it's not even *at* a church," Becca protested. "This time we're meeting right here in the school auditorium."

"Yeah, and I don't know how you get away with using a public high school for a religious group," Solana grumbled.

"The school can rent space to any community group willing to pay the standard fees," Becca reminded her. Her face brightened. "Now that basketball season is over, The Edge can use the gym!"

"Well, you go and have a good time," Solana told her. "I've got better things to do on a Friday night than listen to some judgmental Christians telling me what's wrong with my life."

"Have you ever heard the speakers at The Edge?" Becca challenged. "Seems to me you're the one being judgmental—you're so sure you know what they're going to say without even giving them a chance." She raised her eyebrows. "Besides, what do you have to do on a Friday night these days?"

"Ouch!" said Solana. "That hurt."

"Sometimes the truth does," Becca said, smiling to take the sting out of her words. On the nights the rest of the group went to The Edge, Solana would usually have a date—usually a different guy every time. But then she met Ramón and starting spending every possible moment with him—including weekend nights. Becca knew Solana was serious about Ramón when Solana stopped hanging out with the Brio group at Becca's house on Fridays. When Solana and Ramón broke up, Solana swore off guys for a while. Becca knew she'd probably be sitting home alone tonight.

"Come on, Sol," Becca urged. "It wasn't so bad at Crazy Charlie's, was it?"

"Thanks, but no thanks," Solana said, with a finality that let Becca know the subject was closed.

• • •

"Go, Becca!"

Becca smiled through gritted teeth as she heard Tyler's voice above the roar of the crowd. She was crouched and ready to receive the tap from her relay teammate. Tonight's competition at The Edge was probably the best yet, she thought. She could hardly believe her eyes when she walked into the gym and saw the incredible obstacle course that was set up. She'd literally held her breath when the competitors—two boys and two girls—were announced for each team. She had whooped out loud when her name was called.

The course was set up in duplicate so that two teams could compete side by side. Four of the six teams had already gone, and their times were posted on the scoreboard. Becca shot a glance at

Nate, who crouched at the other starting line. Like her, he was in the anchor position for his team. Becca wondered whether he noticed that Tyler was cheering for her, not for him.

Nate looked over and flashed the grin that always sent Becca's stomach on a roller-coaster ride. "May the best man win," he shouted over the noise of the crowd.

"Or woman," Becca shot back. She saw with satisfaction that her teammate was well ahead of Nate's. As soon as she felt the tap on her shoulder, she took off.

The first obstacle was a rope climb. Becca's arms were strong from rock-climbing, so she swarmed up the rope as fast as a pirate climbing a mast in one of Tyler's beloved old movies. A song from *The Pirates of Penzance* came into her head and gave her a good rhythm for her hand-over-hand climb.

At the top of the rope was a mesh bag holding Nerf balls. Every competitor had to shoot one through the basketball hoop on the end wall of the gym. Failure to make a basket added 65 seconds to the team's time, so each competitor had to strategize. If they missed the first shot, was it worth their time to take a second shot? What about a third? How many shots could they take and still leave enough Nerf balls for the team members behind them?

Becca reached into the bag. Two balls left. No problem. She'd been shooting hoops with anything she could find—basketballs, paper wads, balloons—since she could walk. Squeezing a Nerf ball, she took aim, automatically compensating for the lightness of the ball. *Swoosh!* Nothing but net.

As Becca slid down her rope, she passed Nate climbing up his. She'd have to move fast if she wanted to keep the lead she'd started with.

The next obstacle, a series of barrels to crawl through, was to her advantage, though. She knew Nate would have trouble fitting his broad shoulders through the last, smallest barrel. She emerged ahead of him and easily dribbled a soccer ball around the orange cones.

She sprinted to a ladder and climbed to reach the knotted end of a rope that was draped over the top rung. With one foot still on the ladder, Becca positioned her other on top of the knot at the bottom of the rope. This was the trickiest part of the course: She had to swing on the rope, Tarzan-style, and grab another ladder suspended horizontally about 15 feet away. From there, to reach the finish line, all she needed to do was to cross hand-over-hand as if she were on the monkey bars in a playground.

Taking a deep breath, Becca pushed off the ladder and squeezed both feet together above the knot on the rope. With one hand she clung to the rope while she reached out with the other for the opposite ladder.

Yes!

She grasped the first rung. As she let the rope swing away, she heard Nate let out a jungle yell behind her, so she guessed he was swinging on his rope. She resisted the urge to look back and see if he was pounding his chest. Instead, she concentrated on the finish line.

"Bec-ca! Bec-ca! Bec-ca!" her team chanted as she swung from rung to rung beneath the ladder. At this point in the course some of the other competitors had gotten tired and slowed down—one girl had even dropped off the ladder and had to start that section of the course over. But Becca was too pumped to feel tired. She was so close!

"Go, Nate," a segment of the crowd yelled, and Becca glanced at the other lane. While Becca's smaller size had been an advantage in the barrels, Nate's height and strength were definitely an advantage now. With long, easy swings, he reached over three rungs at a time. He was even with Becca, then ahead.

Becca gave it all she had, but she could see she was beat. Nate dropped to the floor when Becca was only two-thirds of the way across the monkey bars.

As soon as she hit the floor, her team mobbed her.

"Way to go, Becca!"

"You were awesome!"

Becca caught Nate's eye as his team hoisted his lanky 6'3" frame to their shoulders. "Great job," she shouted, giving him the thumbs-up sign. "But wait till next time!"

Jacie and Tyler pushed through the crowd to reach Becca and Nate so they could walk together to the auditorium for the rest of the program. Jacie had Hannah's wrist in her grasp. "She won't shove," Jacie explained. "She'd be left behind if I didn't hang on to her."

"Then Nate better hold Becca's hand," Tyler teased. "'Cause he sure left her in the dust."

Becca made a face at him, and Nate laughed out loud. "One thing I never worry about is Becca keeping up with me!" But he took her hand anyway, bending down to say softly in her ear so that no one else could hear, "You're one girl worth hanging on to."

"Like an electric fence," she murmured, then laughed at Nate's startled expression. "Never mind," she said as they started toward the auditorium. "It was just something Solana and I were talking about."

Solana. If only she had come tonight. She'd love it—it's fun; it's loud; and our friends are all here. Becca frowned. *I should have talked her into coming. I really failed.*

"Becca! Great job on the obstacle course!"

Pulling herself out of her private thoughts, Becca looked into the smile-creased face of Michelle Roberts, one of her youth leaders from church.

"You didn't waste a second making that basket," Michelle continued. "No wonder your team picked you for anchor."

Becca grinned. It was just like Michelle to pick up on the part of the course that Becca was most confident about. She was good at noticing details like that. *When some people give you compliments*, Becca thought, *they're so general that you don't know if they really mean anything. But Michelle pays attention.*

"So how come you looked so down just now, Becca?" Michelle asked. "Not because you came in second, surely—even if it is hard to come in behind this guy," she added, flashing a smile at Nate.

"Did I look down?" Becca was surprised.

"Kind of like this," Michelle said, and pulled her face into a frown. With a mischievous twinkle she pressed her fist against her mouth, and Tyler roared with laughter.

"She's got you, Becca!" he said. "You do that all the time without even knowing it."

Becca gave a sheepish grin. *Michelle pays better attention than I realized*, she thought.

"I guess I was thinking of failure," Becca admitted.

"Second place isn't failing," Hannah said quickly. "Most girls wouldn't have been able to do nearly as well." Becca had to smile. Coming in second in the race didn't bother her at all, but it was sweet of Hannah to be so loyal—even if Becca didn't agree with the implication that girls couldn't be as athletic as guys!

"Failure," Michelle said thoughtfully. She gave a nod—the quick, definite little nod that Becca thought was probably as much a part of Michelle as her unruly hair and the laugh lines around her mouth. "That's hard."

Something about the way she said it made Becca think that Michelle had more serious things in mind than an obstacle course. Impulsively, Becca said, "Michelle, do you have time to talk?"

"Always," Michelle replied with another nod.

"I mean now?"

"Sure," said Michelle.

"We'll go save some seats in the auditorium," Nate suggested, giving Becca's hand a squeeze before he let go. "Look for us toward the middle where we usually sit."

I do like that guy, Becca thought. *I couldn't stand being with a guy who would hang all over me, but Nate always seems to know when I need some space.*

"Want to go someplace quieter?" Michelle asked. The hallway was still jammed with students moving noisily toward the auditorium.

"Let's try the quad," Becca suggested, leading the way to a table in the courtyard in the triangular center space created by the sides of the school buildings. She sat down on the table and put her feet on the bench.

Michelle perched on the edge of the table next to her and leaned toward Becca, her elbows on her knees. "Failure," she said reflectively, picking up the conversation. "Are you talking about sports?"

"No," Becca said.

"I didn't think so," Michelle said, with a quick smile. "I've never seen you let losing a game get you down. You just seem to work harder the next time."

"Exactly!" Becca agreed. "But with some things it doesn't seem to matter how hard you try."

"You've got something pretty important in mind," Michelle suggested.

"Yeah. It's my friend Solana." Becca looked at Michelle. "Do you remember her? She never comes to youth group or The Edge, but I think you met her at one of my games."

Michelle nodded.

"Well, she's not a Christian, and it seems like no matter what I do to try to share my faith, she's just not interested. I couldn't even get her to come here tonight." Becca gave a discouraged sigh.

"And that makes you feel like a failure," Michelle said.

"You got *that* right!" Becca exclaimed. "Hannah practically told me it was my fault if Solana goes to hell," she added bitterly.

Michelle raised her eyebrows. "Wow. It can get pretty messy when you start mixing up your job with the Holy Spirit's."

"Huh?" Becca frowned. "I don't get what you mean."

"When you care about somebody the way you care about Solana," Michelle explained, "it's easy to start thinking it's your job to get her saved."

"Isn't it?" Becca asked.

Michelle just looked at her and waited.

Becca thought a minute, then said, "You mean it's the Holy Spirit's job to get Solana saved, don't you?" Michelle nodded, and Becca went on. "But then what's my job?"

"Why don't you tell me?"

Becca rolled her eyes. "To share my faith. To pray for her. To be a good example."

"Why do you say it like that?" Michelle asked. "As if it's such a dumb thing to say?"

"Because it's such a Sunday school answer!" Becca said.

Michelle smiled. "Don't you think sometimes 'Sunday school answers' can be true?"

"But it doesn't work!" Becca burst out. "That's the whole problem. It doesn't matter how much I share my faith and pray and try to set a good example. It just doesn't work."

Michelle was silent for a few moments. She seemed to be gazing into the dark corners of the quad as if she'd find answers there. "Yeah," she said finally. "I guess that's why it's called *faith*. Because we're supposed to keep believing even when we don't see any results."

But I want *results*, Becca thought. *And I believe God does, too.* She sat silently, thinking about what Michelle had said, until one of the quad doors swung open and spilled a rectangle of light from the hallway onto the grass.

"What are you doing out there?" a voice called from the doorway. "It's time to be in the auditorium."

"It's okay, Mark—we'll be there," Michelle called back.

"Oh, sorry! I didn't know it was you, Michelle," the man said apologetically. "I was afraid it was some couple sneaking off." He closed the door.

Michelle laughed. "Mark's a youth leader at Heritage Church, and some of the kids in his group broke a window at their last lock-in. Not just any window, either; it was a stained-glass picture of Jesus as the Good Shepherd. Mark really got it from the church board for not keeping closer track of his group. I bet he'll be patrolling the halls all night just to make sure nobody from his group gets into any trouble."

Becca stood up. "I'm ready to go in anyway. I was hot from the obstacle course before, but now I'm kind of cold."

"We didn't really solve anything about Solana, did we?" Michelle said as they walked across the quad.

"No," agreed Becca.

"Sometimes we have to let things remain unsolved. It's not easy."

"No kidding," Becca said, wishing that weren't true. But that's one thing she really liked about Michelle. She was always honest and said things like they were. She didn't pretend to have answers when there weren't any. "Thanks for listening."

"Any time," Michelle said.

When they reached the auditorium, a band was playing, and students were clapping and singing along.

"There's your friends," Michelle said. She pointed to the center section and Becca spotted Nate, standing tall and waving at her, with Jacie bouncing up and down beside him to attract her attention. "See you Sunday," Michelle said, giving Becca a hug before she headed off to talk with some other students from Becca's church.

Becca slid into the row beside Nate and looked around the auditorium, watching people and checking out who was there. Up front near the band, a group of younger students were bouncing on their feet, their hands pumping toward the ceiling. One of them spun around in a fast dance move, and Becca recognized Hannah's brother Micah. She wondered whether Hannah's parents knew Micah could dance like that. *Probably not*, she thought. *They probably don't know he's here with Kelli Hendricks, either.*

Hannah's parents were committed to courtship, not dating, for their children, but Micah didn't necessarily see eye-to-eye with them on that subject.

Becca turned to watch Hannah. She was always amazed at how Hannah's self-consciousness fell away in a worship setting. It was as if the Christian music gave her a freedom to move and express herself that she didn't feel any other time. Right now Hannah stood with her eyes closed, face upturned, swaying in perfect time to the music. Tyler was watching her. He caught Becca's eye and shrugged, raising one eyebrow and giving the quizzical half-smile that was his trademark way of letting people know he didn't take himself too seriously. Becca smiled back. She knew Tyler so well that she could guess that he was reliving the infatuation with Hannah he'd had when she first came to Stony Brook High this past fall. He certainly was disappointed when Hannah reaffirmed her commitment to courtship.

The band finished playing and everyone settled in the theater-style seats to listen to the speaker. Nate slouched in his seat, his knees on the back of the seat in front of him and his broad shoulders even with Becca's.

"Are you a risk-taker?" the speaker began. "What kind of risks are you willing to take for what's really important?"

Her attention immediately captured, Becca leaned forward and rested her elbows on her knees. *What's really important to me right now?* she asked herself. Immediately her thoughts flashed to Solana and the picture Becca had posted on her bulletin board. *Reaching Solana, of course!* she thought. *Not that there's anything risky about that. Or . . . is there? The same old things we've been trying don't seem to be working. Maybe that's the risk—daring to find some new way to get through to Solana.* Becca smiled in anticipation. *I'll keep my eyes open for any chance that might work,* she decided. *Risks don't scare me!*

chapter 9

"Man, Katie, you work us harder than Coach does," Becca panted as she threw herself on the grass. "With all these sprints you have us running, you'd think we were training for track, not for basketball."

"You'll thank me next March, when we take the state championship," Katie said confidently.

"Are we going to do this every Saturday till March?" another junior on the team complained.

"Don't worry," Katie assured her. "This Saturday is only to make up for missing Monday's drill."

"Good," said Becca, "because I go to the community center on most Saturdays."

"And I like to sleep in," added another girl.

"Tell you what," suggested Katie, "let's plan on no less than once a week from now till school's out, just to keep our teamwork strong. Once summer vacation starts, we'll see what works."

The girls murmured their agreement and started packing up their gear to go. Becca remained sprawled on the grass, and Katie sat down next to her.

"I've got you pegged as a starter next year, Becca," Katie said.

"Don't you think the coach will want to have some say in that?" Becca asked, but she was pleased just the same.

"Oh, I think she'll agree with me," Katie said.

Becca raised herself up on one elbow and looked at Katie curiously. "What makes you so confident?" she asked. "Like this whole off-season training thing—how did you get everybody to go along with it?" She wondered whether Katie might have some secrets of persuasion. Becca often wished she had some way to persuade people to do something—like get Kassy to make dinner on Becca's night, or get Solana to help at the community center, or go with them to The Edge.

"Well, it just makes sense, doesn't it?" Katie replied. "The division rules limit the months we can practice as an official team with our own school coach, but there aren't any restrictions on getting together on our own. It didn't take much convincing to get the rest of the team to see that."

"Well, you're doing a great job," Becca said sincerely. "I don't think I could have pulled it off."

Katie was silent a moment, then she said quietly, "I think you could, you know. You just have to tap into your spiritual resources."

"Mmm," Becca murmured, thinking this over. "Were you at The Edge last night? The speaker talked about the spiritual resources you need to take risks."

"No," Katie said with a smile. "The Edge isn't really my scene." In answer to Becca's inquiring look, she explained, "I don't really need some guy up front telling me what's what."

"That's how Solana feels about it too," Becca said. "But The Edge isn't like that."

"Solana's pretty strong-minded, isn't she?" Katie said with a chuckle.

"You got that right," Becca agreed. "She had a good time talking with you at the gallery, though." She paused, thinking about the cleanup. "How are Willow and Raven doing? Do they need more help?"

"No, but thanks for asking," Katie said. "Some of Raven's friends have been helping out this week, and they've pretty much got the shop back together."

"I'm so glad," Becca told her. "I'm surprised they were able to reopen so quickly."

"Willow is grateful that you and your friends came to help—they wouldn't have been able to do it without you."

"We were happy to do it. And it was nice getting to know Willow a little better."

"Yeah, Willow's great." Katie's face brightened. "No matter how crazy things get—like with this flood and all—she just stays really calm and centered."

"Maybe I ought to hang around her more and see if it would rub off on me," Becca joked. "Calm" was about the last word anybody would use to describe her when her life got too stressed.

"You could come along with us tonight if you want," Katie suggested. "Willow and I are going on a midnight hike to see the full moon—are you interested?"

"Sure." Becca had just been kidding about spending time with

Willow, but she wouldn't mind it—and she loved hiking by moonlight. The stars were amazing to look at away from the city lights. She loved the night sounds, the cool evening breeze, the sense of adventure. "I bet Solana and Jacie would like to come too. Would that be okay?" *I won't even ask about Hannah*, she thought. *There's no way her parents would want her out in the woods in the middle of the night.*

"Sure, they can come," Katie agreed. "But no guys. Tonight is strictly a girl thing."

"No problem," Becca said. "That'll be great with Solana right now!"

At home, Becca got her parents' permission to go on the hike, then called Solana and Jacie to invite them.

"With Katie and Willow?" Jacie asked, when Becca got her on the phone. "Why don't we just go by ourselves?"

"But I already told Katie I'd go with her," Becca protested. "What do you have against her and Willow?"

"Nothing . . . exactly," Jacie said. "I just . . . oh, I don't know, Becca. I just didn't like being with them on Monday, I guess."

Becca didn't know what to say. Jacie usually liked everybody.

"Thanks for asking me, Becca," Jacie finally said, "but I think I'd rather not go."

Solana, on the other hand, was eager to have something better to do than sitting home moping about Ramón. She was full of enthusiasm when Becca picked her up. They ran around Copper Ridge until eleven when they drove to the trailhead where Katie had said to meet. It wasn't far from the trail they had been on the day of the flood, but Becca had never been on this particular one before.

Katie and Willow were waiting for them as they clambered out of the car and slung their knapsacks on their backs. Becca thought both girls seemed as buoyantly expectant as she felt.

"Why is hiking by moonlight so much more special than by daylight?" she wondered aloud, automatically speaking in a low voice, even though there was no one to be disturbed for miles around.

"It could almost make you believe in magic, couldn't it?" Solana asked as they hiked along a path dappled with moonlight and shadow.

Katie laughed. "Could a scientist like you believe in magic?" she teased.

"Probably not," responded Solana. "But," she went on, and Becca heard a note of enthusiasm in her voice, "the Native Americans who first settled here thought there was something special about this area. Not magical, but sacred."

"That makes sense," murmured Katie.

Becca looked at her curiously. "What do you mean?"

Katie paused for a moment. "I mean I can understand this being a sacred place a long time ago, because it feels like a sacred place to me, too," she explained in a careful voice. "I feel closer to the Lord when I'm out in nature." She looked at Becca as if she was trying to gauge Becca's reaction, and Becca wondered whether she was looking for a signal about how much she could say without antagonizing Solana.

"Oh, no! No God talk, please!" said Solana in a disgusted voice.

"You started it," Katie pointed out. "You're the one who said this was a sacred place. If the Native Americans had a sense of the spiritual, why shouldn't we?"

"When I look at all this—" Willow gestured at the trees

around them and the stars and moon just visible through the branches above, "I'm positive there's a creative power in the universe."

The heavens are telling the glory of God, thought Becca, quoting Psalm 19 to herself.

"Creative power isn't necessarily the same thing as God," Solana challenged.

"I think of God as a beautiful, many-faceted diamond," Katie said. "Depending on where you are and where you're looking, you see different aspects. Creative power—that's one aspect of God."

They came to a fork in the trail, and Katie stopped. "Well . . . ?" she asked Willow.

Willow appeared to consider the unspoken question for a moment, then nodded.

"Well, what?" Solana demanded.

"We were just wondering which trail to take," Katie explained. "Some other friends of ours are out here tonight, and we were wondering if we should take you to meet them or go on the other trail." She smiled at Becca. "I'm sure they'd like to meet you. They've been praying for your friend Otis."

Becca felt a pleasant little glow inside. It was good to know that Katie wasn't the kind of person to say she'd pray for someone, then forget all about it. She'd even asked her friends to pray for Otis!

"You're not taking us to some midnight prayer vigil, are you?" Solana asked suspiciously.

"What do you know about midnight prayer vigils?" asked Willow in a surprised tone.

"My family's Catholic," Solana said. "They used to drag me to midnight Mass, Easter vigils, the whole works, when I was little."

"Don't worry," Katie assured her. "Nobody in our circle would try to drag you into anything. We totally do not agree with forcing our beliefs on anybody."

"Then I'm okay either way," Solana said. "We can meet your friends or take the other trail—whatever you want. What do you want to do, Becca?"

"Let's meet the others," Becca said. She was curious about this group who was praying for Otis.

Katie led them up the trail to the left, and after about 20 minutes Katie stopped at the edge of a clearing. "Hail!" she called out.

"What's she talking about?" Becca whispered to Solana. "It's not hailing."

"Not *hail* as in *hailstones*, you illiterate," Solana whispered back. "*Hail* as in the old-fashioned way of saying hello."

As Katie slowly led them into the clearing, Becca thought the scene in front of her did look like something from another time and place. Eight or nine girls stood in a circle in the center of the glade. The moonlight streaming down unimpeded by trees illuminated the circle almost as brightly as if it were day, but with a silvery, almost dreamlike light. Several of the girls wore their hair long with ribbons entwined in it, and one had a garland of evergreen on her head. Becca wondered if the needles made her head itch. The girl in the center of the circle held a long-stemmed rose in her upstretched hand. The full moon looked so large and close that it almost seemed as if she could touch it.

"They look like flower children from the sixties," Becca said to Solana in a low voice.

"No," Solana answered, "they look like something out of those Sir Frank Dicksee posters Jacie has all over her studio."

"Yes!" Becca agreed in sudden recognition. "The ones of Romeo and Juliet, and that lady on horseback with flowers in her hair."

As they approached the circle, the girl with the rose lowered her arms and moved gracefully to meet them. Parting the circle with a smooth gesture of her hands as if she were drawing back curtains, she smiled at Katie. She touched Katie on the forehead with the rose, and the circle widened and Katie took a place on the perimeter. The rose girl, as Becca thought of her, did the same with Willow, and Willow took her place in the circle.

Whatever Becca had expected Katie's friends to be like, it wasn't this. Having ribbons and roses on a hike was just plain weird. On the other hand, it was so beautiful with the full moon shining into the center of the circle that she wondered who came up with this pretty way to enjoy a night in the forest. It was so serene and almost, well, *holy*—at least to Becca. She let the weirdness fall away and decided she would just enjoy the beauty of it all.

Solana cast a questioning look at Becca. Becca gave her a smile and shrugged, and Solana stepped up to the circle.

"Welcome into our circle," said the rose girl, touching Solana on the forehead and drawing her in.

Smiling at Becca, she reached out with the rose again. "Welcome into our circle."

chapter 10

"Jacie, you should have come! You would have loved it!" Becca burst through the door of the shack that served as Jacie's studio, already in mid-sentence before Jacie even looked up from her sketchpad.

"Slow down, Becca! You've lost me already. What would I have loved?" Jacie tucked a wayward curl behind her ear and fixed Becca with the I'm-giving-you-my-full-attention look.

"Everything," Becca said, flinging her arms wide in an extravagant gesture and flopping into Jacie's old upholstered rocking chair.

"I would have loved everything?" Jacie said, her dark eyes starting to twinkle.

"Absolutely," Becca agreed emphatically. "It reminded me of Alyeria, you know?"

"Not yet." Jacie shook her head.

"Not yet what?" Becca asked, confused.

"Not yet—I don't know what reminded you of Alyeria," Jacie said. "Why don't you just tell me from the beginning?"

"That's what I'm doing," Becca said. "I'm telling you about the night hike last night."

"Ah! Now I get it," Jacie said. "Keep going."

"It was really cool," Becca said, picking up an apple from among the clutter of paint tubes and charcoal pencils on Jacie's worktable and tossing it in the air. "Can I have this?" When Jacie nodded, she took a big bite and began to talk around it. "Katie and Willow brought us to this place they go up in the foothills above Crystal Springs."

"That's what reminded you of Alyeria?" Jacie said.

"Yep," Becca nodded as she took another bite of apple. When she and Jacie and Solana were in elementary school, they had invented an imaginary world they called Alyeria. They played elaborate games of make-believe in a secret spot in a grove of aspen trees on the school grounds. It had been a girls-only game until the day in fourth grade when Tyler had crashed in on them, waving a stick for a sword and challenging Becca to a duel. He had fit into their imaginary world so well that he became an accepted part of the group from then on. As the friends grew up, Alyeria came to represent more than just childhood games; it stood for their friendship and their accountability to one another. Even now, if Tyler or one of the Brio girls was having an especially hard time, the friends would gather in the aspen grove to be together and give each other support.

"You know how when we're in Alyeria, it's different from being someplace ordinary, like my family room," Becca said. "It's like the place shapes how we act together."

"Like this?" Jacie picked up her sketch book and started drawing with rapid pencil strokes. Becca wanted to get up and look at her sketch, but she knew Jacie's "rules" about her artwork: no looking at it until Jacie was ready to show it. Jacie sketched quickly, then held up the page for Becca to see.

"Mmm, that's Alyeria, all right," Becca said. In a few simple strokes, Jacie had captured not only the appearance but the mood of the group one of the last times they were in Alyeria. A tousle-headed Tyler, his face obscured by a shock of hair falling over one eye, was slumped against a fallen log. Jacie sat on one side of him, her head just resting on his shoulder, while Solana sat on the other, one hand on Tyler's arm. Becca sat with her back against Tyler's, but while Jacie had sketched the other girls with fluid lines, she had drawn Becca with short, straight pencil strokes that somehow managed to convey a sense of strength and purpose.

"You have such a gift, Jacie," Becca said sincerely. "This picture brings back exactly how I felt right then. I'd been kind of mad at Tyler—"

"*Kind* of mad?" Jacie interjected. "You were about ready to wage a one-woman war if he took up with Jessica again, as I recall."

"Three-woman," Becca corrected. "You and Solana would have been right with me if he'd started going with that cat."

"Kindness, Becca," Jacie warned.

"Well, anyway," Becca said, "I was mad at Tyler for letting Jessica take over his life, but then when everything fell apart for him, it was like all the energy I'd been spending on anger just refocused into being strong for Tyler. When we sat there in Alyeria, I felt like I was sending him my strength." She studied the sketch again. "How did you catch that in this drawing? I didn't think you even knew what I was feeling then."

Jacie nodded. "Sometimes when I draw or paint, I see things I didn't know I knew. It's happened before."

Becca shook her head. "Amazing." She looked intently at the sketch again. "You and Tyler look almost like boyfriend and girlfriend."

Jacie snatched the sketchbook back and glared at the picture. "No, we don't!" she said, tearing the page off the pad. She shoved it under a pile of other loose pages and turned back to Becca. "You were telling me about this place on the hike that reminded you of Alyeria," she said, changing the subject. "Tell me about it, and I'll see if I can sketch it."

Eagerly, Becca described the events of the night before. As she talked, Jacie sketched, looking up from her page now and then to let Becca know she was listening. When Becca's narration finally wound down, Jacie held up the page to show Becca what she had drawn.

"That's cool," Becca exclaimed. "It's not exactly the way things really looked, but you got the feeling just right." She glanced from the sketch pad to the poster of a medieval lady on horseback that was on the wall. "Solana said it looked like something out of one of your Sir Frank Dicksee posters. Look." She pointed to the woman on horseback. "You've drawn her face on the girl with the rose."

"*La Belle Dame sans Merci*," Jacie murmured.

"Huh?"

"The beautiful woman with no mercy," Jacie translated. "It's the name of the painting. I wonder . . ." Her voice trailed off. "I think I'd like to paint this."

"Oh!" exclaimed Becca, suddenly remembering. She pressed her fist to her mouth. "The thing is—" She stopped, embarrassed.

"What?"

"Would you mind not showing it to anybody?" Becca said.

"Why not?" Jacie seemed surprised. "You're the one who's always telling me I *should* show my work."

"I know," Becca agreed. "It's just that Katie kind of asked us to keep it a secret."

"Why?" demanded Jacie. She leaned forward to grasp Becca's wrists and looked her straight in the eye. "Were they doing something wrong up there?"

"No!" Becca said, returning Jacie's gaze frankly. "What could be wrong?"

"I don't know," Jacie admitted. Her grip on Becca's wrists was gentler now, but she seemed troubled. "Drugs?"

"No way!" Becca pulled her hands free to punctuate her points in the air as she talked. "First of all, you know I'd never mess with drugs. Second, Katie's an athlete. She'd never fool around with that stuff, either. And neither would any of the other girls."

"How can you be so sure?" Jacie asked quietly. "Do you really know any of them?"

"Besides Katie and Willow, not really," Becca said. "I did recognize a couple of the other girls from school, though. There's a girl named Kara—she's a freshman. I've seen her hanging around some of the partiers at school," Becca admitted, "but that doesn't mean she's a spacer herself."

Jacie looked unconvinced, and Becca could sense her concern.

"Don't worry, Jacie," she said. "I know there weren't any drugs there. These girls are super-wholesome—kind of back-to-nature types, you know?" She laughed. "They didn't even want me to drink the Mountain Dew I brought along—we all had fruit juice and whole wheat crackers!"

"What's the big secret, then?" Jacie persisted.

Becca shrugged. "I guess they don't want a lot of other people barging in on their special place, the same as we don't let just anybody into Alyeria. I mean, we don't even let Hannah into Alyeria. It's not that we don't like her, or that we have some dark secrets going on—we just have our own special place."

"But they let you and Solana in," Jacie said.

"Yeah, and that's the best part," Becca said. "Jacie, I really think these girls could talk to Solana about spiritual things, and she'd listen. She seems really interested in Katie's group, and she knows that they pray and stuff. Willow was talking to Kara about how important it is to have daily devotions to keep yourself centered, and later I saw Solana asking her questions about it."

"What did she say?" Jacie asked.

"I couldn't tell. They were talking really quietly and I decided it was better if I didn't try to listen in." She shook her head regretfully. "Solana doesn't seem to want to hear what I have to say about faith, you know?"

"Yeah, I know," Jacie agreed. She looked sad. "Why would she listen to Willow instead of her own best friends? We've been praying for so long for her to meet Jesus."

"Maybe this is how God is finally answering our prayers," Becca said, her eyes shining. "Maybe these girls can reach Solana even though we can't."

"Maybe," said Jacie doubtfully. "Do me a favor, though, Becca. I know you like to jump into things with both feet, but find out a little more about this group before you get in over your head, will you?"

"I told you, Jacie—they aren't doing drugs." But when she saw how truly concerned Jacie looked, Becca relented. "If it will make you feel better, I'll talk with Katie about it."

chapter 11

"Becca, wait up!" Katie's voice rang out over the clamor of slamming lockers and noisy chatter as students flooded the hallway after the final class period of the day. "Unless I'm interrupting something?" she added with a question in her voice, looking from Becca to Nate.

"Nope. Just walking to the parking lot," Nate said. "Walk with us."

"No—I've got to stop in the athletic office before I go home," Katie replied. "But first I wanted to get Becca's opinion on a new training drill I'm working on."

"You go ahead," Becca said to Nate. "I've got some stuff I want to talk with Katie about, too."

"Okay. See you later," Nate said, running one finger lightly down Becca's hair. "I'll call you tonight."

"Watch out, Becca," Solana said, coming around the corner just in time to see Nate touching Becca's hair. "You know what static electricity will do to your hair." Turning to Katie, she explained, "Nate's got this electric fence thing going for him."

Becca smiled as she watched Nate's long strides carry him down the hall while Solana and Katie chatted a moment. Then she leaned against the lockers next to Solana and turned her attention to the training drill Katie wanted to talk about. She felt flattered by how much attention Katie was giving her lately. Becca really admired Katie's athletic ability, and it felt good to know that Katie respected her opinions on the off-season training program.

I remember how much I felt like an outsider this fall when I decided not to go out for the volleyball team, Becca thought. *It feels good to be part of the inner circle now.*

"What did you want to talk to me about?" Katie asked after they'd worked out some of the details of the new training drill.

"I was wondering about your friends I met on the night hike," Becca said. It had been a couple of weeks since the hike, and although Katie seemed interested in developing a stronger friendship with Becca and Solana, she hadn't asked them to do anything more with the other girls. "Is that like a prayer group, or part of your youth group, or what?"

"What she wants to know is if they do drugs," Solana said bluntly.

Becca felt her face get hot. *I shouldn't have told Solana that Jacie was worried about that*, she thought. *I should have known she'd blurt it out. I'm glad at least that I didn't tell her that Jacie did a painting from the sketch of the full-moon hike. She'd probably tell Katie about that, too, and then Katie would really be mad at me*. "That's not what I meant," she began, but Katie just laughed.

"Don't worry about it! We're not druggies—we're just a circle of friends who get together to try to become better people—and make the world a better place," Katie said.

"I like that," Becca said, and Solana nodded in agreement.

"If more people were serious about making the world a better place, we wouldn't have the environmental problems we have now," Solana said.

"Too many people just *talk* about the problems," agreed Katie. "They don't believe their actions could make a difference."

"And you believe we can?" asked Solana.

"I *know* we can," said Katie with conviction. "With Spirit power."

"Yeah?" said Solana skeptically. "I don't feel too powerful compared to those mining companies that are ready to tear up the mountainside just to make a few bucks."

"You have to know how to tap into the power, that's why," Katie said, and Becca held her breath. At this point, somebody like Hannah would launch into the four spiritual laws or something equally "churchy," and Solana would tune right out. What would Katie say next?

Katie seemed to be thinking about what she would say next too, because she was silent for a moment or two. "Are you really interested in this?" she finally asked, looking from Solana to Becca.

Now it was Solana's turn to consider. "*Interested* might be too strong a word," she said at last, "but I guess I'm curious."

"We have a kind of special gathering this Saturday night," Katie said. "Sort of to celebrate the first of May."

"A May Day party?" Solana said. "Do you remember how we used to have to dance around those stupid May poles in gym class when we were in elementary school? Becca used to weave left when she was supposed to weave right and tangle up all the ribbons. She made the gym teacher crazy."

"Careful what you make fun of," Katie said. "Sometimes I still dance around a May pole on the first of May."

"Right," Solana said, clearly not believing her. "And that's what you want us to do Saturday?"

"No," Katie said, turning serious. "Spring is a season of rebirth, so we take time to reflect and make a fresh start."

Solana nodded her head thoughtfully. "I guess everybody needs a fresh start sometime," she said, and Becca wondered whether she was thinking about starting over after her relationship with Ramón.

"I know I do," Katie affirmed. "This week I'm writing down all the negative things I've done. If I can, I try to make things right."

"How do you do that?" Solana asked.

"Well, by apologizing to people I've hurt, or paying back favors I've taken for granted—that sort of thing."

"What if it's something you can't undo?" Solana asked bleakly.

"Then I try to learn from my mistake," Katie said. "On Saturday, we'll all burn our lists to show that we're done with those things and are starting over with a clean slate."

Becca nodded. She had done that same sort of thing on a youth group retreat last year. She remembered the sense of utter relief she felt as she watched her list of sins burn up in the campfire and heard her youth leader read promises about forgiveness from the Bible. *If only Solana could have that same sense of peace over the things she did with Ramón*, she thought.

"Where are you getting together?" Solana asked Katie. "On

that same trail where we went on the full-moon hike?"

"No—we're meeting at Willow's house. I can draw you a map if you want to come," Katie offered.

"I wish I could," Becca said regretfully, "but I've got something going with my own youth group on Saturday night." She decided not to mention that her youth group was playing laser tag. Laser tag was a blast, but it sounded kind of superficial compared to Katie's plans.

"How about you?" Katie asked Solana. "Do you want to come?"

Solana hesitated. "It's sounds cool," she said. "Kind of—I don't know—healing."

Katie nodded. "It is."

Solana still seemed undecided. "Maybe I'll wait till sometime when Becca can go, too," she finally said.

"Oh, Solana, don't skip it just because of me," Becca urged quickly.

"It's no big deal, Becca," Solana said. "Don't worry about it."

But it is a big deal, Becca thought. *At least it could be if this helps you see what it means to be forgiven*. Aloud she said, "Let's both go. I can miss my youth group this one time." *Michelle will understand*, she decided, smiling as she always did when she thought of her favorite youth leader. *She's always telling me to put people before projects*.

"Here's how to find Willow's house," Katie said, sketching a quick map in her spiral notebook. She tore the page out of the notebook and handed it to Becca. "You can't miss it."

"You don't know Becca," said Solana, reaching for the map. "I'll take that. Becca would get lost. What time should we be there?"

"Eight," said Katie, turning to walk toward the athletic office. "Oh, and one more thing . . ."

"Yeah?"

"Don't tell anyone else about it."

"Why not?" Becca asked, recalling Jacie's worries about drugs.

"It's not as pure if you start telling people what you're doing. It's kind of like bragging about how you're getting morally clean."

"Oh, yeah. I guess that makes sense." *Kind of like the Pharisee who wanted everyone to know how repentant he was*, Becca remembered. "Okay. I won't tell anyone. Except my mom and dad, of course."

"Becca, I really have to ask you not to talk to *anyone* about this. We all agree to keep it private."

"Well, sure. Of course I wouldn't say anything about what people put on their lists and stuff," Becca agreed. "I just meant I need to tell my mom and dad where I'm going."

"Well, okay—if you have to," Katie said. "Just don't go into details about it. It'll be much more powerful if it's your own personal experience." She headed off down the hall. "See you later!"

"What are you going to write on your list?" Solana asked Becca as they walked toward the stairway leading down to the parking lot.

"I don't know yet. It's not the kind of thing I usually sit around and think about, you know?"

"You don't usually sit around and think—period!" Solana teased as Becca sprinted down the stairs. "This will be good for you."

Becca made a face. "You make it sound like getting a shot." She pretended to pull back the plunger on a syringe and advanced on Solana as she spoke in a falsetto voice. "This is going to hurt a little, but it will be good for you."

"Spare me the bedside manner," Solana laughed. Then her face got serious. "You might not be so far off," she said. "I think making this list *might* hurt a little. But I think it'll be good for me."

chapter 12

JOURNAL

things i'm sorry for:

- not telling otis more about jesus
- having an attitude about hannah sometimes
- having so much fun having an attitude about hannah
- forgetting devos
- certain daydreams about nate
- telling kassy she's a spoiled brat, although she does get away with doing hardly any chores around the house
- taking my good life for granted when so many people don't even have a place to sleep at night
- deceiving mom and dad

Becca erased the last item on her list. She wasn't really deceiving her parents; she just hadn't gotten around to telling them that she was going to Willow's tonight instead of to youth group.

On the other hand, when her mom had told her to have a good time at youth group, Becca hadn't said anything to let her know she wasn't going. Becca penciled the entry back on her list.

But if she was really sorry for deceiving her parents, part of this whole list deal was that she would make up for it. And how could she do that without telling them she'd been deceptive? Then she'd have to explain about keeping the gathering private, and she'd be breaking her word to Katie . . .

It's not like I'm doing anything they'd disapprove of, she thought as she erased the entry again. *I'm just keeping a friend's secret. That's all.*

She heard a pounding on her bedroom door and shoved her list into her pocket.

"Don't knock the door down, Kassy," she yelled. "I'm coming!"

"How'd you know it was me?" Kassy asked, walking into the room and dumping an armload of stuff on the bed.

"It was either you or a charging elephant," Becca said. "Who else knocks so hard that the neighbors check their doors?"

"Sometimes you don't hear," Kassy explained, unfazed. "Okay—let's get you ready." She started sorting the pile on the bed.

"Get me ready?" Becca echoed. "What are you talking about?"

"You're going to play laser tag, aren't you?" Kassy said, as if that explained everything.

"Uh . . ." Becca stalled. "What does that have to do anything?"

"You gotta wear black for laser tag." Kassy held a black leotard up to Becca's chest and looked at it critically. "You're much harder to see if you wear black."

"I'm not wearing your leotard!" Becca exclaimed, taking it from Kassy's hands and dropping it on the bed.

"Why not? You're not that much bustier than I am," Kassy said with an air of self-satisfaction. "I'm sure it would fit."

"I don't need—" Becca bit off her sentence. *This secrecy thing is getting complicated*, she realized. *If I tell Kassy I'm not playing laser tag, she'll pester me till I tell her where I'm going. Then she'll blab it to Mom and Dad.*

"You don't need what?" Kassy asked impatiently. She had gotten up and was rummaging through Becca's closet.

"I don't need to look like a ballerina for laser tag," Becca improvised. *That's true*, she thought. *Sort of.*

Kassy frowned. "Please, Becca. I'm a gymnast, not a ballerina." She held up a pair of black Lycra warm-up pants she'd unearthed from a pile on the closet floor. "Put these on."

"Kassy," Becca started, then sighed. It was easier to give in. "Okay, but no leotard."

While Becca pulled on the pants, Kassy flipped through the pile she'd dumped on Becca's bed.

"How about this?" she offered, holding out a black leather jacket with a triangular tear in one sleeve. "I found it in Matt's closet."

Becca slipped it on.

"You look like a biker chick," Kassy said approvingly.

"I look like I'm playing dress-up," corrected Becca, checking herself in the mirror. "These sleeves hang practically to my knees."

"Work with me, Becca," Kassy said in an exasperated tone. "You're not even trying."

Becca sighed. "Okay—what's this?" She picked up a soft heap of fabric and shook it out.

"That might work," Kassy agreed. "Mom got it for one of those city council hearings when she wanted to look severe. Try it on."

Becca let Matt's jacket fall to the floor, then shrugged out of her cotton sweater and slipped the black shirt on. It was tailored like a man's dress shirt with long tails that came halfway to Becca's knees, but the fabric was soft and flowing. "At least it's comfortable," she said.

"Turn around," Kassy commanded, and Becca obligingly pivoted for her inspection. "Just right," Kassy pronounced. "Now just let me accessorize you."

"*Accessorize* me?" Becca threw out her arms to ward off her sister. "I thought the point was to *camouflage* me."

"Your problem is you have no fashion sense, Becca," Kassy said, evading Becca's defensive gestures and deftly tying a sheer black scarf around Becca's ponytail. "You could really look good if you'd only try."

"Thank you for that vote of encouragement," Becca said dryly. "Are you finished with me yet?"

"Uh-huh," Kassy said. "Unless you think maybe a black choker . . ."

"I do *not*," Becca said firmly. *I'm going to feel silly enough as it is going to Willow's house dressed in Kassy's version of the perfect laser tag outfit.*

"Then I'm going to go tell Mom you're borrowing her shirt. I'm sure it'll be okay." Kassy waltzed out of the room, leaving the discarded clothes scattered on the floor.

"Uh, Kass," Becca called, "were you thinking of picking up after yourself?" But Kassy was already halfway down the stairs. "Typical," Becca muttered, stepping over Matt's jacket on her way out of her room. She stopped, suddenly remembering. Turning back, she retrieved the list from her jeans pocket and tucked it in the breast pocket of her mom's shirt, then followed Kassy down the stairs.

"Doesn't she look great, Mom?" Kassy said as Becca headed out the door. "I wish I could go with you," she told Becca with a note of wistfulness in her voice. "You always do such cool things."

● ● ●

When Becca walked into Willow's house, her first thought was, *Raven must be her own best customer*. The room Willow led them into looked as if it had been decorated from Raven's shop. Candles burned in groupings around the room, and a large yellow pillar candle glowed in the center of a slate-topped coffee table. Arranged on the tables were other items from the gallery: a silver unicorn rearing on an amethyst-colored crystal, an intricate weaving with beads and feathers, a really lovely ceramic bowl with lotus-shaped candles floating in it, and what seemed to be a dish of white bath salts.

The girls Becca had met on the full-moon hike were already there, seated on the floor around the coffee table. They seemed to be in the middle of a discussion, and Becca shot a quick glance at her watch, wondering if she and Solana were late.

Eight o'clock, she noted. *That's when Katie told us to come*. But it seemed clear that the others had been there for a while—there was none of the chit-chat and getting settled that Becca would have expected if the group were just getting started. *I wonder if they started earlier but there was something Katie didn't want us here for,* she thought. *Maybe they do their prayer time, or some Bible study, right at the beginning, and Katie knew that would turn Solana off.*

Katie was sitting on her knees by the table, but when Willow led Becca and Solana across the room, she rose and came to greet them.

"Welcome into the circle," she said to each girl. She dipped her finger into a little ceramic pot she held in one hand, then touched it to each of their foreheads. Becca saw that the spot on Solana's forehead glistened in the candlelight, and when she inhaled, the fragrance reminded her of being in the bath and body shop at the mall.

"Jasmine scented oil," Katie explained. "Isn't it nice?"

Becca sat down and glanced around the circle. She had to press her fist against her mouth to suppress a smile: It seemed that Kassy's choice of laser tag apparel was just as appropriate here. Willow was wearing the artsy-looking black tunic Becca had seen her wear to school a few times, and two or three of the other girls were wearing similar outfits. *I fit right in*, Becca thought. *It must be the gallery look.*

"We were just talking about our lists," Katie said to Becca and Solana, "and Kara had some questions." She smiled encouragingly at the slim, dark-haired girl to Becca's right.

"I was wondering if it was right to put something on my list or not," Kara began hesitantly.

"There are no rules you have to follow with your list," Katie said. "There's no one right way to do this."

"It's okay to follow your own path," Willow put in.

"Well, I'm confused. Do you think sex is a bad thing? Is that something to write on my list?"

Out of the corner of her eye, Becca saw Solana lean forward.

"Sexuality is a good thing," the rose girl from the night hike said.

"But people can abuse it," countered a girl across the circle.

"It's so easy for people to get hurt," Willow said. "And anything that hurts someone is wrong."

"Harm no one," the rose girl said to Kara. "That's really the main thing to remember."

"I thought what I did sexually wasn't hurting anyone," Kara said tearfully. "But it ended up hurting me. I feel as if I have a big hole right in the middle of my heart."

Solana got up from her place in the circle and moved to sit next to Kara. Becca scooted over to make room.

"I know what you mean," Solana said, taking Kara's hand in hers. "Oh, I know just what you mean."

"Sexuality *is* good," Becca said to Kara. "It's part of how we're made. But sex outside of marriage is wrong. That's what you're feeling now."

"For you, sex outside of marriage is wrong," the rose girl said to Becca. "But you can't force that opinion on someone else."

"I can't make someone else believe it, if that's what you mean," Becca said, "but that doesn't make it any less true."

"But what Kara needs right now is healing, not judgment," Katie said quickly. "So Kara, if you want to include a past sexual experience on your list, you can burn it and put it behind you." Katie gestured to the tall yellow candle on the slate table.

Kara wiped her eyes and gave a little trembling smile. Becca saw Solana give her a squeeze of encouragement before she let go of her hand. Kara slowly got up and walked to the table. She held the corner of her list in the flame, then dropped the burning paper into a ceramic bowl Katie held out to her. Almost immediately, Solana followed.

Becca felt a sudden surge of gladness as Solana's eyes met hers over the candle. Solana gave Becca the barest hint of a smile, then focused her attention on her list. With a look of resolution on her face, Solana lit the paper and dropped it into the bowl. Becca heard her sigh as she straightened her shoulders. *She's serious about making a new start*, Becca realized. *She wants something new—a new way of life, I hope! I'm glad I came—I'm so glad Solana and I can do this together!*

With a feeling of anticipation tingling in her stomach, Becca rose and joined Solana to burn her own list.

● ● ●

Later, while the girls were enjoying juice and pink-iced spice cupcakes, Becca pulled Katie aside.

"Thanks for inviting us tonight," she said.

"I'm glad you came," Katie answered. "I hope it meant something to you."

"Oh, it did!" Becca said. "Only . . ." she paused, wanting to get her words straight so she wouldn't say anything to offend Katie. "I don't get why you cut off the discussion about sex without making it clear what God's plan is—that sex is only for within marriage."

"Why would you expect me to do that?" Katie asked.

Becca was startled. "Well, isn't this group supposed to be—" She stopped, suddenly wondering just how to describe what she meant.

"Supposed to be what?" Katie prompted.

"Well, I mean, I know you pray together sometimes, and I've heard people talking about devotions, and so I thought this was sort of an alternative type of Bible study." Even as she said it, Becca realized she hadn't seen anyone else with a Bible—but then, she hadn't thought to bring her own Bible, either.

Katie gave her a look Becca didn't quite understand. "No, it's not a Bible study," she said. "It's a group for people at all different places on their spiritual path. Most of us have been in the circle for a while, but Kara's been here only once or twice more than you and Solana have. She's just finding out about us."

"I understand about making things open to people who are still checking out the faith," Becca said. "The Edge does that too. But don't you think you still have to be clear about what you believe?"

"Becca, what you heard tonight *is* what I believe." Katie smiled at Becca's expression. "Now you're shocked. But I told you before, I'm not into some kind of religion where somebody else tells me what's right and what's wrong. We don't just buy into everything they try to teach you in church. We're not into getting dressed up on a Sunday morning and going to a huge building that looks like a converted gymnasium with a movie screen in front. Or some little building with stained glass windows, either—what's the point of those anyway? We want to find our spiritual path for ourselves."

Becca suddenly felt the way she did the first time she went rappelling and stepped over the edge of a cliff into thin air. She had thought she knew where she stood with Katie and her circle, but now she wasn't sure.

"What are you saying?" she finally asked. "I thought you were like a student-led youth group. That's why I brought Solana. I hoped she'd get interested in the faith."

"I think Solana is getting interested," Katie said. "But she's not necessarily buying into everything you mean when you say 'faith.' She's checking it out for herself." Katie paused. "You know, Becca, that wouldn't be a bad thing for you to do. You can think for yourself, girl. You don't have to swallow everything you've been taught."

chapter 13

"Did you have a good time last night, Honey?" Becca's mom asked as Becca dragged herself into the kitchen Sunday morning. "Sorry we didn't wait up for you, but Dad and I were both exhausted."

Becca opened her mouth to pour out her confusion to her mom, then abruptly shut it again. *How can I ask her all my questions when she thinks I was off playing laser tag? If I tell her where I was, she'll know I lied to her and Dad. I can't deal with that right now.*

"Really interesting," she said. *That's true, anyway,* she thought. "I, um, I met some new girls." To avoid further conversation, she made herself very busy with the Sunday paper.

"Grab some breakfast while you read the paper, Hon," her mom said. "I'm going to hop in the shower, and then it'll be time for church." She dropped a kiss on the top of Becca's head as she left the kitchen.

Phew! At least while I'm alone nobody can corner me into fibbing about last night, Becca thought.

"Hey, Becca!" chirped Kassy, dancing into the kitchen and grabbing a bagel off the counter. "How was laser tag? Did anybody say anything about your outfit?"

"Oh—it was great," said Becca, faking a smile. "The outfit was great, I mean. It was just the right thing to wear."

Kassy nodded with satisfaction and Becca dashed out of the kitchen. She passed her dad and Alvaro, lying on their stomachs on the family room floor with the comics section between them, and rushed to her room without saying another word to anyone. *I'll stay here till it's time to leave for church*, she decided, ignoring the grumbling in her empty stomach.

Normally Becca loved her church and the youth Sunday school class, but today she couldn't seem to focus on the message or the worship. Three high school students gave a report about a missions trip they'd taken during spring break.

"I never knew how sheltered I was until I saw what life is like in Mexico City," one of the guys said. "I guess I just took for granted how much we have in America because that's the way I grew up."

Is that what I'm doing with my faith? Becca wondered. *Am I taking for granted that it's right because that's the way I grew up? Is Katie right?* she kept asking herself. *Am I just accepting everything I've been taught, or do I really believe all this?*

As she was leaving the sanctuary after church, Michelle Roberts caught her by the elbow.

"Can I talk to you a minute?" she asked.

Uh-oh, Becca thought with a sick feeling in her empty stomach. *She's going to ask me why I wasn't at laser tag last night*. Looking around to make sure her parents were out of earshot, Becca reluctantly nodded at the youth leader.

"At our staff meeting last week, we brainstormed some student leadership projects," Michelle said, "and your name came up. I wondered if I could take you out for coffee—or hot chocolate," she corrected herself, knowing Becca didn't like coffee. "So we can talk about it."

"Sure," Becca said. "That would be great." She was so relieved about not being in trouble for skipping youth group that she would have agreed to scrub urinals with Michelle—which, come to think of it, she'd done a few times at the community center.

On Tuesday Michelle picked Becca up from school and took her to Copperchino. "The usual?" she asked, and ordered a mocha hot chocolate for Becca and a latte for herself. They settled into two curve-backed chairs at a small table and Becca took a gulp of hot chocolate, burning her tongue as she always did.

Michelle put both elbows on the table and leaned forward. Her face was eager, and Becca could almost feel the waves of enthusiasm radiating from her.

"I'm excited about some new ideas we have for our youth ministry," Michelle said.

"You're always excited about something," Becca accused her.

"You're probably right." Michelle laughed, and the smile lines around her mouth deepened. "I hope you're going to be excited too." She opened her eyes wide in a way that seemed to invite Becca to join her delight at what was to come next.

With infectious enthusiasm she described a plan for

mobilizing students from the youth group to start student-led ministries in their high schools.

"You guys know better than anyone else what your friends are looking for—what issues they're struggling with, what questions they're asking. Questions they might never ask their parents or a youth leader."

Becca nodded. That part hit pretty close to home.

"We want to use the leadership gifts of Christian kids to meet some of those needs. With guidance from adults, of course. But I really believe that God can use teenagers just as much as He uses adults—or even more."

She briefly highlighted what she called the theological grounds for the plan, which made Becca smile—Michelle was the only real-life person she knew who got excited about theology.

"Of course, accountability is important for every leader, no matter what age," Michelle said. "So we've outlined three requirements for these student leaders: to be a committed Christian and able to articulate their faith; to be active and faithful in church and youth group; and to be willing to be accountable to the church's youth board." She looked at Becca. "Do all those make sense?"

"Uh-huh," Becca said. "You wouldn't want kids who aren't strong Christians trying to lead others."

"Exactly," said Michelle. "And we don't want students leading on their own because it's too easy for them to get burned out or go off track. We want them to always have someone to keep an eye on things and be available for questions or help. That's why it's so important to keep connected with church."

Becca nodded to show she understood, but inside she was thinking, *That's exactly the kind of attitude Katie would hate. The idea that kids need to have somebody else watching everything they do and keep them on track.*

She pulled her attention back to realize that Michelle was running through a list of possible ideas for student-led ministries ranging from spearheading service projects based in the high school to leading before- or after-school Bible studies.

"What I *really* like about this," she concluded, and Becca grinned, because Michelle "*really* liked" every aspect she'd mentioned so far, "is that this kind of ministry doesn't just make an impact in the school." She widened her eyes as she looked at Becca. "It *really* makes an impact on the student leader." She gave one of her quick, emphatic nods. "I can't begin to tell you how being a youth leader has impacted my faith." She smiled. "Well, let's say I could begin but I wouldn't know where to stop."

Michelle sat back and gave a deep sigh, as if savoring everything she had just talked about. Then she leaned forward again and fixed Becca with a wide-eyed gaze. "So what about it? Are you ready to take this next step and become a student leader?"

Becca just gaped at her. She realized she should have known Michelle was leading up to this, but she'd gotten so caught up in Michelle's explanation that she was taken completely off guard.

"You'll want to pray about it, of course," Michelle said with another of her quick little nods. "But I can tell you that I've been praying about it for a while now, and I really think God has equipped you for this. I feel that even more strongly after our conversation about your friend Solana. I think it's the kind of challenge you need to keep growing."

"I . . . well, yeah, sure I'll pray about it," Becca stammered. Inside, she was thinking, *What's wrong with me? Two months ago I would have been all over this. But now . . . Now I'm not sure this is the right place for me. I'd hate to disappoint Michelle, but . . .*

"Becca?"

Becca snapped her attention back to Michelle. "Yeah?"

"It's okay to say no if that's what you decide." She reached out and covered Becca's hands with hers. "Don't let me railroad you just because I'm passionate about this idea. You need to make up your own mind."

"Yeah," said Becca. "That's what I've been thinking."

"All I ask," said Michelle, "is that whatever you decide, you tell me your reasons for your decision."

Becca nodded, but said nothing. *The problem is*, she thought, *I can't tell you my reasons, because they're all tied up in the secrets I'm supposed to be keeping.*

• • •

"So," Katie said, flopping down on the grass alongside the track, "you wanted to talk."

"Yeah," said Becca. "I want to know more about your group."

"My circle?" Katie said, looking at Becca intently. "Why?"

"Because I'm half-involved with it already, and I need to know what I'm getting into," Becca answered. "I've been thinking a lot about what you said about making up my own mind—but I don't know enough about your circle to make up my mind yet."

"Fair enough," Katie said. She plucked a blade of grass and began tearing it into thin strips. Rolling over onto her back, she looked up at the sky. "There are four main principles we follow: to know, to dare, to will, and to be silent."

"Go on," Becca said. "To know what?"

"To know means we're always searching for the truth and we're strong in our beliefs."

Searching for truth—that's what the Bible is all about, Becca thought. *And being strong in what you believe—Christians believe in that too. Although . . . that would depend on whether what you believe is true or not.* "Exactly what are your beliefs?" she asked.

"Hang on," Katie said. "Let me tell you about the other three first. To dare means we're not afraid of the unknown, and that we dare to be different and learn as much as we can."

Becca thought about herself—*daring* was probably a word most people would use to describe her. Paragliding, climbing, looking for adventures—those were all ways of being daring in one sense. And daring to be different was a big value to her, from the way she dressed in thrift-shop clothes to the way she dared to speak up about her faith. *The speaker at The Edge challenged us to dare to take risks for what's important*, she remembered. "That sounds good," she said. "Go on."

"Third one: to will," Katie continued. She paused, as if she was thinking of the best way to express it. "This one's really important. To will means we concentrate on being the best we can be. And changing things around us for the better."

"Okay," Becca said. She thought about her volunteer work at the community center. *I can buy into this one. Christians are definitely supposed to be helping others, taking care of God's world—yeah, changing things for the better.*

"The last one is to be silent. You've already done some of that," Katie said. "That means we don't talk about our spirituality to people who won't be supportive."

"But don't you think it's important to share your faith?" Becca asked. Even as she said it, though, she realized that until recently she'd never even known Katie was interested in spiritual things at all. It hadn't come out much in the years they'd played together on sports teams.

"It's not my job to try to make somebody believe it," Katie said.

Whoa! thought Becca. *That's just what Michelle told me about Solana!* "The first time I heard you talk much about, you know, spiritual things, was at Raven's gallery," Becca recalled. "Is Raven someone who's 'supportive of your faith'?"

"Raven is my spiritual mentor," Katie said. "She's my goddess mother."

"Your godmother?" Becca asked, thinking she'd misunderstood.

"No, my goddess mother. She's training me in the Craft."

"Craft?" Becca had a wild image of Raven and Katie sitting in the gallery weaving dream catchers, but she had a bad feeling that Katie wasn't talking about that kind of craft. "Katie, what exactly *is* your religion?"

"I thought you knew by now, Becca. It's Wicca."

chapter 14

"Oh, boy!" said Becca, bolting upright. "I've gotta go!"

"Chill, Becca!" Katie said, putting a hand on Becca's arm to keep her from going. "You act like I just told you I'm a vampire."

"Close enough! You did just tell me you're a—a witch, didn't you?"

"I prefer the term Wiccan," Katie said calmly, "but yes, basically I am a witch. What's your problem with that?"

"What's my problem?" Becca yelped, pulling her arm from under Katie's hand and edging a foot or so away. "Witches are . . . are . . ."

"Are what?" Katie said. "Look at me and tell me what I am."

"Well, maybe not you, but witches generally are . . ."

"Evil?" Katie supplied.

"Yes!" Becca agreed.

"Not true. The first rule of witchcraft is 'Harm no one.' What's so evil about that?"

"But doesn't Wicca involve worshiping the devil?"

Katie gasped in horror. "NO! We won't have anything to do with evil or the devil." She shivered.

"But don't witches do spells?" Becca persisted.

"Yep," Katie said. "So did you."

"Me?" Becca's voice came out in a squeak. "I never did any spells!"

"Sure you did," Katie persisted. "When you made that list and burned it, that was a spell for ridding yourself of guilt. And you did it inside the magick circle."

"I did *not*," Becca declared. "I had no idea that's what was going on."

"I can't necessarily make you believe it," Katie said with a mischievous glint in her eye, "but that doesn't make it any less true."

"There is no way that was a spell," Becca insisted. "We did almost that exact same thing in my youth group."

"See? Your faith and mine aren't as far apart as you thought."

Becca was horrified. "How can you say something like that? You don't even believe in God!"

"Yes, I do," Katie said in a patient voice. "And I believe in the power of prayer, and in doing daily devotions, and helping others. Don't you?"

"You know I do," Becca answered. "But . . . then what's the difference between Wicca and Christianity?"

"That's a question you ought to answer for yourself," Katie said. "But personally, I don't have any problem with either one. What I *do* have a problem with are Christians who tell lies about my religion. The kinds of lies that make you automatically assume

Wicca is evil. Or those Christians who shove their way down people's throats saying Christianity is the only way."

Becca felt herself blanch. "But don't you reject Christianity?" she asked.

"Not at all! I respect all religions."

"How does that work?" Becca said. "How can you respect them all if yours is the right one?"

Katie shook her head pityingly. "I didn't say my religion was the right one. Or at least, not the only right one. How can you say there's one right way to worship Spirit? That's like saying you know all there is to know about it."

"But there *is* one way," Becca said, finding something to hang on to in those words. "Jesus is the Way."

"I agree."

"You can't agree!" Becca pounded the ground with her fist. "You're a witch!"

"Becca, I really don't think you should try to tell me what witches do and don't believe until you know a little more about it. I'm the witch here, right? So can we agree that I'm the authority on witchcraft?"

"This is getting too weird," Becca said. "I can't believe I'm sitting here talking religion with a witch."

"Well, get over it," Katie said. "But at least I think you're starting to understand why one of our principles is to be silent. I told you about Wicca, and you're totally flipping out."

"I am *not* totally flipping out," retorted Becca. "I'm only slightly flipping out. Which, if you ask me, is a perfectly reasonable response to discovering that the alternative youth group I've been going to is secretly a . . . what do you call yourself?"

"A circle," Katie said. "Or a coven, but I prefer circle. And it's not all that secret. I called it a circle from the very first time I told you about it."

"So all those girls I met at Willow's house—are they all witches?"

"Part of being silent means that I'm not necessarily going to name names, just so you can go off on a, well, a witch hunt," Katie said. "But to answer your question, no. Not all those girls are witches. Some are just checking it out, like you and Solana."

"We are *not* checking out witchcraft!" Becca declared, stiffening her back. "I'm a Christian."

"You don't have to give up Christianity to check out Wicca," Katie said. "You've already seen how much the two have in common—prayer, devotions, God, helping others. You like being out in nature and working to be in harmony with others. And, Becca," Katie looked her in the eye, "Wicca can give you the power to make a difference."

Becca shook her head. "I don't know about that."

"I do. Why do you think we did so well in basketball this year?"

"Talent. Determination. Hard work. Good coaching." Becca looked defiantly at Katie. She wasn't sure she wanted to hear what Katie was going to tell her.

"And the work I did in the circle," Katie said with quiet confidence.

"I don't believe it," Becca said.

Katie smiled. "I can't make you believe it, but that doesn't mean it's not true."

"Okay, you can quit using my own words against me," Becca fumed. "Anyway, if you can get us to the championship with some magick spell, why are we working our tails off with practice and conditioning?"

"If you can pray for the homeless, why do you volunteer at the homeless shelter?" Katie countered.

"Because it would be cheap to pray and not put my money where my mouth is," Becca answered.

"Same thing in Wicca," Katie said. "You have to walk your talk."

Becca shook her head. "You've got me so confused I don't even know which side I'm arguing on anymore," she complained.

"We don't have to argue," Katie said. "I'm just trying to help you understand that what you've been told about Wicca isn't very accurate. People misrepresent what they don't understand. But you don't have to swallow everything you've been told. Think for yourself on this one."

Think for yourself. That's what Michelle told me. That's what I tell Hannah when she spouts out her endless supply of Christian clichés. After all, I don't want to be some mindless Christian.

"You don't have to decide anything right now, you know." Katie broke into Becca's thoughts. "If you want to find out more, you can come to our circle again on Saturday." She got up to leave, then offered a parting inducement. "I could teach you some long-distance healing prayers you could say for your friend Otis."

chapter 15

Becca swerved to avoid another bump in the rutted dirt road that led to Jacie's studio. *I'm going to have to wash this car when I get home*, she thought as the tires kicked up clouds of dust, *or Mom will never let me borrow it again.* She checked her watch. Jacie had told her to come at 4:30; she was right on time.

Why 4:30? Becca wondered as she put the car in park and turned off the ignition. *Jacie doesn't usually have any sense of time when she's drawing or painting.*

She got out and was about to slam the door when another thought crossed her mind. *My birthday is in less than two weeks. Maybe she's giving me a surprise party and that's why I needed to come at a certain time*. Becca smiled at the mental picture of her friends crouched and hiding in the shack, waiting to leap out and yell, "Surprise!" *Not likely*, she decided. *But maybe I'll honk to warn them just in case.* She played a lively rat-a-tat-tat on the horn before slamming the car door and marching up to the shed.

"Surprise!" Becca yelled when Jacie opened the door.

Jacie blinked. "What do you mean, surprise? I asked you to come."

"Nothing. Just an inside joke. I've been feeling edgy lately and I needed to blow off some steam." Becca stepped into the shed and looked at Tyler sprawled in Jacie's rocking chair. "Just Tyler," she observed. "Kind of a small party." She laughed, but Tyler and Jacie remained serious.

"Have a seat, Becca," Tyler said, standing to let Becca take his place in the rocker.

Sobered, Becca sat and looked from Tyler to Jacie. "What gives?" she asked. "I'm starting to get a bad feeling about all this politeness."

"We wanted to talk to you about that painting I did of the full-moon hike," Jacie said, settling herself on the ottoman and gazing intently at Becca.

"We?" queried Becca. "That was supposed to be secret."

"Yeah. Well, I showed it to Tyler," Jacie said. "Sorry." She didn't look the least bit sorry.

"Where is it?" asked Becca, looking around the studio for the canvas.

"I destroyed it," Jacie said, still in the curiously uninflected voice she'd been using since Becca arrived.

"You destroyed it? Jacie, that was a really good painting. What did you destroy it for?" Becca couldn't read any signals from Jacie. *What's going on here?* she wondered.

"I destroyed it because it was a painting of a Wiccan ceremony," Jacie said flatly.

"Oh." Whatever Becca had expected, it wasn't this. She wasn't prepared to defend her venture into Wicca to Jacie and Tyler, however accidental it had been. She tried to think of something to say. "How did you know?"

"You're not surprised?" Tyler said. "You knew it was Wicca?"

"I just found out," Becca said. "I didn't know it when I went, that's for sure."

"And you're not ever going again." Jacie made it a statement, not a question.

Becca ignored Jacie's command. "How did you figure out it was Wicca?" she repeated. "Have you been talking to Katie?" Maybe if Katie had told Tyler and Jacie the same things she'd told Becca, they wouldn't subject Becca to an inquisition.

"No," Tyler answered. "Jacie had a weird feeling about the painting, so she talked to me about it."

"When I painted it, something came through that I didn't even know was there," Jacie said. "Some sense of danger, or evil. Every time I looked at it, it creeped me out. My own painting!" She shuddered. "So I showed it to Tyler."

"Even though I told you it was supposed to be secret," Becca said.

"Some secrets shouldn't be kept," Jacie said simply.

"Anyway," Tyler interjected, "I didn't really get what was bothering Jacie, but a couple nights later I was surfing the Web and I came across this little independent film that was getting great reviews. So I went to the Web site and read the description and looked at the clips and—bingo!—there it was: the whole thing with the moon and the rose and everything. And I found out it's a Wiccan ceremony called 'drawing down the moon.' "

"So he called me and we came here right away," Jacie said,

picking up the story. "And we destroyed the painting."

"I still don't understand why you destroyed it," Becca said. "I thought it was just as good as the posters you have on the walls."

Jacie brushed away Becca's art critique and got back to what was clearly for her the main point. "Becca, you're fooling around with witchcraft! Do you have any idea how dangerous that is?"

Becca shifted uncomfortably in the rocker. Part of her agreed with Jacie, and part of her wasn't sure anymore. And mostly she wanted to defend what she'd been doing. "It's not really what you think, Jacie," she said. "I was there, you know. I saw the thing with the rose and the moon. It was actually kind of sweet."

"Sweet?" Jacie gasped, and Tyler let out a snort.

"Well, you know—like a fantasy. There was nothing sinister about it."

"You're the one having a fantasy if you think you can mess around with witchcraft," Tyler said bluntly.

"You don't understand," Becca insisted. "I wouldn't get anywhere near real witchcraft." She stopped, remembering that Katie *had* admitted that Wicca was a form of witchcraft. "But Wicca isn't what you think of when you think of 'witchcraft,' " she explained, as much to herself as to Tyler and Jacie. "They pray, and they do devotions. There's a lot about it that sounds a whole lot like Christianity. I don't know everything about it, of course," she added honestly, "but I asked Katie a bunch of questions, and it really sounds like a lot of it's okay."

"I don't care what Katie's been telling you," Tyler said. "It's not safe—and it's *not* okay. It's against everything God tells us. I don't know how deep you're in, but you've got to get out."

"I'm not *in* at all," Becca said. "I just went on a hike and to a meeting." As soon as she said it, she knew it was a mistake.

"You went to a Wicca meeting?" Jacie exclaimed. "Becca, what were you thinking?"

"I didn't know it was Wicca. I was thinking I'd go with Solana. We've been praying for her for so long. So when she wanted to go to what I thought was a youth group meeting—"

"How could you think that?" Jacie asked.

"There was nothing to make me think otherwise," Becca retorted. She was about to tell Jacie about burning their sins, but remembered her promise to keep it a secret. "They were having a meeting that sounded a lot like stuff we've done at our youth group. I couldn't *not* go if Solana was interested."

"Maybe you should have asked some serious questions about the group before you went," Tyler suggested.

"Maybe I thought I'd see what it was about before I made any snap judgments," Becca said, more sharply than she intended. "Look, guys, I'm starting to feel guilty until proven innocent here. I'm not doing any witchcraft." A sudden stab of guilt pierced her as she thought about the list-burning that Katie said was a spell. "And I don't need you jumping down my throat."

"I'm sorry, Becca," Jacie said, and this time she sounded as if she meant it. She inched the ottoman closer to Becca's chair and looked into her eyes as if looking into her soul. "We were just so worried about you."

"And Solana," added Tyler, and Becca felt another stab of guilt. It was sort of her fault that Solana had been exposed to all this. *Exposed to all what?* she asked herself suddenly. Just because Tyler and Jacie went all ballistic at the mention of the word "Wicca," she didn't have to get paranoid about it. After all, she had seen it firsthand, and there was nothing scary about it.

"Becca, we didn't tell anyone else about this," Jacie said. "We wanted to talk to you alone—that's only right."

"We didn't even tell Nate and Hannah," Tyler said. "But," he added firmly, "we would have if you hadn't agreed to get out of this Wicca group."

Did I agree to get out of the circle? Becca wondered. *I don't think so.*

"And we're going to hold you accountable, Becca," Jacie added. "And we won't keep silent if we think you need help."

"Help? You make it sound like I'm doing drugs or something," Becca said.

"This is more dangerous than drugs," Jacie said, her face firm with conviction.

Becca forced a smile. "I don't think I was in quite the danger you seem to be afraid of," she said. She looked from one caring, concerned friend to the other. Her frustration and anger dissipated. "I'm glad I have friends who care about me." She looked around the studio regretfully. "I think I would rather have had a birthday party, though."

• • •

That evening Becca's mom knocked on the door of her room after supper.

"Come on in, Mom," Becca called.

"How did you know it was me?" Mrs. McKinnon asked, pushing Becca's algebra book and papers aside to clear a space to sit on the bed.

"Easy. You're the only one who knocks. Kassy pounds, Dad plays a little percussion beat, and Alvaro just bursts in."

Becca's mom smiled. "I noticed that you've been a little unsettled lately."

Unsettled. That's a good word for it, Becca thought. But she wasn't sure she wanted to talk about it, so she didn't say anything.

"So . . ." her mom said after a moment, "want to go for a walk?"

Becca thought. She and her mom had their best talks when they walked in the woods behind their property. Becca knew that asking her for a walk was her mother's way of inviting her to share what was troubling her. And she knew that her mom would listen without criticizing or second-guessing her—that was part of the unspoken agreement when they went on walks. But Becca wanted to think this whole Wicca thing through for herself, without any "right" answers from anybody else. Besides, if she told her mom everything, she'd have to confess to deceiving her about playing laser tag. Becca wasn't worried about getting punished, but she knew her mother would be terribly disappointed. That was almost worse than any punishment.

"No, I guess I'm not in the mood for a walk right now," she said finally.

"Okay." If her mom was hurt, she didn't show it. "Let me know if you change your mind."

I changed my mind, Becca almost said. But her mom was already walking to the door, and Becca bit the words back. She needed to work through this on her own.

Mrs. McKinnon turned, her hand on the doorknob ready to pull Becca's door shut behind her.

"You can always talk to Jesus, you know."

Becca watched the door close. *Maybe I should have told Mom everything,* she thought.

She flopped down on her bed and stared up at the ceiling. *I can talk to Jesus. I guess I haven't done that much lately*. She closed her eyes.

Jesus, I'm confused. I want to have a strong faith—one that other people respond to. Katie seems to have that. People are drawn to her, even Solana. Is what she has a good thing? Something true? Or is it bad, like Jacie and Tyler think it is? Is Katie right that I can learn from her kind of spirituality and still serve You? Is that the way I can reach Solana? And help Otis—if he's even alive. Oh, Jesus, please keep him alive!

I don't know the right thing to do anymore. I told Katie You were the Way. Will You show me Your way?

Becca opened her eyes and lay still, staring at the ceiling.

No answer. Not yet.

chapter 16

"Have you decided whether or not you're coming to the circle this Saturday?" Katie asked Becca and Solana in a quiet voice.

Becca shifted her English book uncomfortably from one arm to the other. She knew she'd have to decide soon, but she still wasn't sure. She glanced at the clock suspended from the hallway ceiling. Two minutes left before her English class started. Maybe she and Solana should just go to class and talk about this later. *As if we haven't just about talked it to death already*, she thought.

"I want to go," Solana said, answering Katie but looking at Becca. When Becca had told Solana that Katie's circle was into Wicca, she had half expected that Solana would blow the whole thing off as superstition. But Solana hadn't; instead, she seemed intrigued.

I asked God to show me what to do about this, and He hasn't given me any kind of answer at all yet, Becca thought. *Unless the fact that Solana wants me to go is some kind of sign.* She frowned unconsciously as Hannah approached them. Hannah didn't know anything about Katie's circle, and Becca wanted to keep it that way. She certainly knew what Hannah would say about it!

"Hi," Hannah said cheerily.

"Hi," Katie said.

"Hi, Hannah," Becca said, trying to sound friendly, but not encouraging her to stay.

Hannah paused as if to stop and join their conversation.

"Can we talk later?" Becca asked, hoping she didn't sound rude.

"Sure," Hannah said, looking uncertainly from Becca to Katie and back. After a second's hesitation she disappeared into the English classroom.

Maybe the way to decide if this circle is okay is to go and check it out for myself now that I know what it's about, Becca concluded, resuming her train of thought. Aloud, she said, "Okay, I'll be there. Just don't trick me into doing any . . ." She stopped. It would be too weird to say "spells" right in the middle of the school hallway.

"Any . . . *workings?*" Katie supplied. "Tell you what, I'll explain everything as we go along if that makes you feel better."

Becca nodded. She was still uncomfortable with the idea that she had been involved with spells at Willow's house without knowing it. But if Katie explained to her what each thing meant, maybe that would be okay.

"Meet us in the grove at eight o'clock Saturday night," Katie said as she turned to go to her classroom, "and you can see the whole meeting from the beginning."

By Saturday night, Becca found she was anticipating the evening's gathering with excitement. Somehow keeping it secret seemed to add to the thrill, as if she were embarking on an undercover adventure. She told her parents that she was going out with friends, and for once she was grateful for Kassy's complaining about how *she* didn't get to do nearly as much fun stuff as Becca—at least it distracted her parents from asking for more details.

Becca was surprised by the number of people in the grove when she and Solana arrived. Besides the eight or nine high school girls she'd seen the last time, she saw several guys her age, and four girls who looked to be about Kassy's age.

"There are guys here!" she exclaimed.

"Why shouldn't there be?" Katie asked.

"Well, it's always been just girls before," Becca said. "I guess that's what I expected tonight."

"We do a lot of things with just girls," Katie agreed. "That's one of the things I like about Wicca—it's not male-dominated like some religions. But there are guys in Wicca too."

"Who are those younger girls?" Becca asked.

"Willow's little sister and some friends," Katie told her. "They're having a sleepover at Willow's tonight."

"Do their mothers know they're here?" Becca asked. She couldn't imagine her mom letting Kassy come to anything like this.

Katie grinned at her. "Does yours?"

Solana gave Katie a nudge. "It looks like something's starting. What do we do?"

"It's time to create the sacred space," Katie said, drawing Becca and Solana toward the center of the clearing where a circle was forming. "Just watch."

Four teenagers stood outside the circle. Each was holding

something, and Becca recognized the objects from the slate table at Willow's house. As the teenagers moved around the circle, Katie whispered in Becca's ear.

"They'll carry representations of the four elements—earth, air, water, and fire—to each point of the compass."

Becca nodded. *The candle is for fire*, she decided. *The feathers must stand for air, and the water is obviously water*. "I don't get what the bath salts are for," she whispered to Katie.

"Salt stands for the earth," Katie whispered back.

Like the salt of the earth? Becca wondered. She still didn't get it, but the four teenagers were chanting something now so she decided to listen to what they were saying instead of asking more about the salt.

"Did they say *angels?*" she asked Katie, in her surprise forgetting to whisper.

"Shh!" Katie warned. "Usually the blessings are silent. But yeah, they said 'angels.' "

Weird, Becca thought. *Angels and blessings and even salt sound like something from the Bible. But feathers? I don't know about that.*

Katie nudged Becca, and Becca realized that the four chanters had joined the circle and everyone was moving clockwise.

"Now we're casting the circle," Katie whispered as Willow called out what sounded to Becca like another blessing. "We always do our working inside a magick circle."

The same four teenagers with the elemental objects began calling out again, and after each one the others in the circle called back a response. Becca looked around to see how many knew what to say. Willow's little sister joined in confidently, she noticed, but her three friends didn't. Becca and Solana were silent, of course, because they'd never seen this part before and didn't know the words. Kara spoke hesitantly, and Becca remembered that Katie said Kara was new to the circle. The chanting took on a musical quality, first softly, then growing louder and louder until Becca felt herself getting caught up in the rhythm even though she didn't catch all the words.

"Now it's time for the invocation," Katie whispered. Becca looked at her in surprise. Her church didn't use the word "invocation," but when she visited her grandparents' church in Illinois, she always noticed "invocation" in their printed order of worship. She remembered it because she'd had to ask her grandpa what it meant. She tried to recall his answer. *Oh yeah—asking for help. That's the part when the pastor asks the Holy Spirit to help the people worship.*

"Who are they invoking?" she asked Katie.

"Spirit," Katie whispered back.

"The Holy Spirit?" Becca said.

"Sure. That's the name you use," Katie said.

This can't be all bad if they're asking the Holy Spirit to be here, Becca thought. She began to relax, then Katie continued, "Spirit is also the Lord and Lady."

"I know the Lord, but what's this about a lady?"

"That's the feminine manifestation of Spirit. Or you can say god and goddess," Katie explained. Becca stiffened at the word "goddess," but Katie simply said, "I told you Wicca isn't male-dominated like some religions. Now watch."

Willow stepped into the center of the circle, accompanied by one of the guys. With almost dance-like moves, she put her right hand over his heart, and he covered her hand with his left. Then he put his right hand over her heart, and she gently placed her hand on top of his. Their flowing motions had an almost dreamlike quality, and Becca found herself swaying gently with the rest of the circle, as if to a silent melody.

She heard a deep sigh and glanced at Solana. She had a longing expression on her face. The scene *did* look romantic, Becca decided. Across the circle Kara had clasped her own hands to her heart, her eyes closed and face uplifted.

"They're asking the Lord and Lady to enter the circle," Katie said in a dreamy voice, directing Becca's attention back to the pair in the center. "Now we'll all draw down the moon."

Drawing down the moon, Becca thought. *What a lovely phrase. That's what Tyler called Jacie's painting*. She looked around the circle, feeling almost as if she were moving in slow motion. "Do we need a rose?" she whispered back.

"No." Katie shook her head gently. "There are many ways to draw down the moon. You can use roses or wands or just your arms. First, we turn to face the moon."

Becca saw that most of the circle had already turned toward the moon, and she obediently followed their example.

"Now raise your arms as if you're grasping the moonbeams," Katie said, extending her arms. "And invite the goddess to enter you."

Becca's arms were halfway up before what Katie said fully sank in. *And invite the goddess to enter you.*

"NO!" Becca yelled, leaping backward out of the circle. "I don't invite anyone into my heart except Jesus!"

"She's breaking the circle!" A concerned murmur ran around the circle, but Becca didn't care.

"Come on, Solana," she cried. Grabbing Solana by the hand, she turned and ran as fast as she could away from the grove.

chapter 17

Becca stumbled as she ran, tears blurring her vision.

"Slow down, Becca!" Solana panted.

Becca scarcely heard her. She clung to Solana's hand, pulling her along, oblivious of the branches that whipped against her face or the uneven trail beneath her feet.

When they reached the fork in the trail, Becca finally came to a stop.

"Becca, are you all right?" Solana took Becca by the shoulders and peered into her teary eyes.

"Oh, Solana," Becca cried, "I almost betrayed Jesus!" In her emotion, Becca forgot about weighing her words so they wouldn't sound too "churchy" to Solana. She just spoke from her heart. "How could I have been so blind? How could I have *anything* to do with a group that would invite anyone except Jesus into their hearts?"

Solana put her arm around Becca and gently led her a little way up the trail that forked off to the right. "Come on, Bec. We'll find a place to sit down for a while."

They moved wordlessly along the trail until Solana spotted a fallen tree and pulled Becca down to sit beside her on it. She waited quietly, her arm around Becca, until Becca's sobs quieted.

"Okay, *amiga*. I'm here for you. You know that," she told Becca. "But what gives? Why did you take off like that?"

Becca took a couple of deep breaths. When she felt as if she finally had her voice under control, she said, "It was that part about asking the goddess into my heart. That's when I knew that Wicca is completely and totally wrong. The only one I ask into my heart is Jesus." She drew another breath that broke into a sob. "Jesus is the *only* person I allow inside me. I was so wrong to think even for a second that I could have both Jesus *and* Wicca. They're entirely different."

Solana gave her shoulder a squeeze. "Don't be so hard on yourself," she said gently. "I don't think you did such a terrible thing." She stopped, and Becca guessed she was looking for some way to comfort her. "If Jesus is all you think He is, He wouldn't mind if you share your heart. You let Nate in your heart, don't you?"

Becca shook her head. "It's not the same at all," she said. "I love lots of people—my mom and dad, Matt and Kassy and Alvaro, you and Jacie and Tyler and Hannah." She smiled, a glimmer of humor coming back to her. "I plead the fifth on Nate. But I don't love you guys the way I love Jesus. That's an exclusive thing."

"That's one of the things that really bugs me about your Jesus," Solana admitted. "This whole exclusive business. It's so narrow-minded. Why does it have to be *only* Jesus? That sounds pretty selfish."

"Jesus isn't selfish," Becca said. "But He *is* jealous."

Solana made a face. "Jealousy—that's ugly."

"It can be," Becca agreed. "But I don't think it always has to be. Sometimes it's right to be jealous."

"Like when?" Solana said skeptically.

"Well, like in marriage," Becca suggested. "Imagine if my dad came home one day and told my mom he was going to marry another wife."

"Never happen," Solana said. "People get divorced, but not your parents."

"No, I mean what if he wanted to be married to my mom *and* somebody else. Have them both."

"That's disgusting," Solana said. "No self-respecting woman would ever stand for that. *I* never would!"

"Even if the guy said he still loved you just as much as before?"

"That would be a lie. If he loved me, he'd be faithful to me," Solana said.

"Exactly," Becca agreed. "It's the same way with me and Jesus."

"But you're not *married* to Jesus!" Solana insisted.

"No, but what I have with Jesus is too important to mess with," Becca said. "Not just important to me—important to Jesus. That's why He gets jealous when I fool around with something else—like Wicca."

"Jesus is jealous over *you?*" Solana asked. "But . . . I mean . . .

He's supposed to be God, right? And, no offense, Becca, but you're just . . . well . . . you."

"I know," Becca said. She blinked back the tears that unexpectedly came to her eyes. "Pretty amazing, huh? That God gets jealous over me."

Solana was silent. Finally she said quietly, "That must make you feel pretty special." She spoke almost wistfully, without the sarcasm Becca was used to hearing when she talked about God.

"It does," Becca agreed. "It makes everything different."

"What do you mean?" Solana asked, as if she were interested in spite of herself.

"It's hard to explain," Becca said slowly. "It's like there's an emptiness inside me that only Jesus can fill. If I have my family, and my friends, and Nate, but when I'm not close to Jesus, I still feel empty. Do you know what I mean?"

Solana was quiet for a moment or two. "Yeah," she said finally. "I guess I do. At least, I know about that empty space inside. Even when Ramón and I were closest, I still felt that emptiness. *Especially* when we were closest," she corrected herself in a sad voice.

Becca nodded wordlessly.

"But I still don't get why you freaked out in the circle," Solana said.

"Because—oh, this is hard to explain," Becca said. "Okay. You're my friend, and I love you. But you're not *really* inside my heart, right?"

"Duh."

"But you see, Jesus is. Well, maybe not literally in the organ that pumps blood, but He's inside the core of my being—the place of control. So inviting the goddess or the 'lord and lady' into my heart means giving them Jesus' place—the place of honor and control over my life."

"So 'in your heart' is a metaphor for saying Jesus is in charge?"

"It's more than a metaphor," Becca insisted. "Jesus can really be inside me—in my will and my mind and the core of what makes me who I am."

"That makes no sense," Solana said.

Becca shrugged. "I suppose it doesn't until you've experienced it. But believe me, it's real."

"And you think this goddess is somebody real, too?" Solana asked. "Somebody who could come in and take control?"

"I don't know," Becca answered honestly. "I do know that there are spiritual beings besides God who would like to be in Jesus' place. I'm not sure what would happen if I invited the goddess to enter me—but one thing I *am* sure of: I don't want to risk it!"

"You'd rather risk losing Katie's friendship?" Solana asked unexpectedly.

Becca pressed her fist to her mouth. "Oh, boy," she said, dropping her hand to her lap. "I guess I've pretty much busted up that friendship." She gave Solana a twisted smile. "But yeah, what I have with Jesus is worth it."

Solana looked Becca hard in the eye. "If it came to choosing between me and Jesus, would you drop me?"

Becca returned Solana's gaze steadily. "I'm pretty sure Jesus would never ask me to drop you—unless I let you begin to control my life."

At that, Solana chuckled, disturbing the stillness of the woods.

"What's so funny?" Becca demanded. "I'm being serious here."

"I was just trying to picture me controlling you," Solana said. "As much as I hate to say this, Becca, I really can't imagine you letting anyone but God control your life."

"What scares me, Sol," Becca said soberly, "is that I almost gave that up." Her expression clouded. "Solana," she said, her voice trembling just a little, "I really need to be alone for a little while. I—" she hesitated, then decided to say it straight out. "I need to talk to God."

"Let's go home," Solana suggested.

"No, I need to talk to God *now*," Becca said. "Before I face my parents or anybody else."

"Becca, it's dark and I'm not leaving you alone in the woods. I'm sorry." Solana sounded as if she really meant it.

Becca thought a moment, then smiled. "Okay," she said. "Then do you mind if I pray right here? Would that be too weird for you?"

Solana snorted. "Weird? After what we've been through tonight you're worried about being weird? Girl, I've seen so much weird in the last two hours, nothing could bother me now!" But she looked a little uncomfortable when Becca slid to the ground and rested her folded hands on the log.

"Tell you what," Becca suggested when she saw Solana squirm, "how about I go up the trail just a little ways. We won't really be leaving each other alone in the woods, but I can be more private."

"Are you really that desperate to, uh, talk to God?" Solana said.

"Yes," Becca answered simply. "I am."

Becca walked a few yards up the trail and settled down cross-legged to pray. Resting her head in her hands, she poured out her guilt and grief.

"God, I messed up big time. I wanted so badly to reach Solana for You that I tried to make it happen on my own. I totally lost my focus on You. I don't know how I could ever have let myself be fooled by Wicca, but I did. I'm so sorry, Jesus, for thinking I could serve You and still experiment with Wicca. I'm so sorry for leading Solana into this. I'm sorry for thinking for one stupid moment that Wicca could lead her to You. Please forgive me."

Becca didn't know how long she spent talking to God, or even whether she was praying silently or out loud. But by the time she walked the few yards back down the trail to Solana, she knew that God had heard her. Better, God had let her know, in some way she couldn't explain, that He forgave her.

"What?" she said to Solana when she reached the fallen log where Solana was waiting. "What's the look for?"

"I'm waiting to see if you're going to glow in the dark," Solana said, but her voice didn't have the sarcastic edge it might have held a few weeks ago.

"Glow in the dark?" Becca repeated, making a face.

"Yeah—you've got that all-lit-up-inside look you sometimes get," Solana answered.

"I do?" Becca thought about it for a moment. Then she shrugged. "I guess I am."

"This God thing is real for you, isn't it, Becca?" Solana said slowly. "You really do have something inside."

Becca smiled. "I do." She hesitated, unsure how much more to say. She felt as if she'd blown things so badly with Solana lately that she wanted to be careful. Finally she just said simply, "You can too."

For once Solana didn't roll her eyes. She stood looking

seriously at Becca. Then she gave herself a little shake, as if pushing the serious thoughts out of the way. "Come on, Miss Glow-in-the-Dark," she said, "show us the way down this trail and back to the car!"

chapter 18

JOURNAL

Dear God,

Becca stared at the words she'd just written for a moment, then put her pen to the paper again.

It feels a little weird to be writing to you like this. But I've decided I need to make this journal a prayer journal, not just a place where I write my thoughts to myself. I haven't done so great on my own lately, so if it's okay with you, I'd like to have you in on this whole thinking and journaling business.

I don't know exactly how to start. I

guess, God, I'm kinda confused. I felt so close to You last night! When I left the circle and spent time with You alone in the woods (well, pretty much alone, except for Solana), I knew You were right there with me. I knew everything was all right between us again.

That ought to be enough, shouldn't it? If You've forgiven me—thank You, Jesus, for forgiving me!—then we don't need to drag my parents into this, do we? I know I've been deceiving them lately about what I've been doing and where I've been going. And I'm sorry for that. But that's all over, I promise.

Becca rolled over on her bed and stared at the ceiling. She really didn't want to tell her parents that she'd been looking into Wicca. She flipped back to her stomach, picked up her pen, and began explaining herself to God.

They'd be so disappointed in me, God. I don't want to hurt them. After all, it's over. What they don't know can't hurt them.

What I didn't know about Wicca could've hurt me pretty bad. The thought came into Becca's head seemingly from nowhere. *And if I don't tell them, won't I still be deceiving them?*

Becca thought about how wonderful she felt last night after

spending time talking with God—"glowing in the dark," as Solana had said. But how different she'd felt this morning when she faced her parents over breakfast. Even in church, which she thought she'd love now that she was back on track with God, she felt uncomfortable sitting between her mom and Kassy—like she had some shameful secret that she had to keep hidden inside.

GOD, IT'S LIKE I'M BUBBLING OVER WITH HOW GOOD YOU ARE, BUT THE ONLY WAY TO SHARE IT IS TO LET PEOPLE KNOW HOW BAD I'VE BEEN. AND THAT WOULD BE WAY TOO HARD.

Becca sighed, then picked up her journal and carried it to her desk. As she opened the top drawer to shove the journal in, the picture of Solana in the center of her bulletin board caught her eye.

"I was off track there, wasn't I, God?" she whispered. "I thought I was being such a good Christian friend, but it shouldn't be Solana in the center. It should be You. I keep trying to do it my way, when it ought to be about Your way."

She crammed the journal into the crowded drawer and shoved it closed. Then she moved Solana's picture a few inches to the right. She pulled her tournament ribbon off the board and gazed thoughtfully at the empty space in the middle of the board. *I want You in the center from now on, Jesus.* She opened the jewelry box on her dresser and dug through the tangle of chains until she found a necklace with a simple silver cross on it. She pushed a thumbtack through the chain so that the cross hung in the center of her bulletin board. *I'll keep this necklace here when I'm not wearing it,* she decided.

She turned to leave her room, then stopped. *Otis,* she thought.

He needs Jesus too—wherever he is. She flipped through a paragliding magazine until she found a photo of a glider that looked enough like Otis's to satisfy her. Tearing the picture out, she tacked it to her bulletin board next to Solana's picture.

"Okay, God," she said aloud. "You're in charge. Please get through to Solana and Otis." Then she headed downstairs.

In the family room, Alvaro was sprawled in a litter of pages pulled from the comics section of the Sunday newspaper. He seemed to be industriously applying wads of bubble gum to his favorite cartoon strips. When he saw Becca he pulled one of the gray globs off the page and held it up for her to admire, and Becca realized that it was Silly Putty, not bubble gum.

"Cool, Alvaro," she said, inspecting the reverse image of Snoopy's friend Woodstock. "I used to do that too. I never did figure out how the picture gets onto the Silly Putty, though."

Becca's dad looked up and smiled from his favorite easy chair, where he was surrounded by the rest of the Sunday paper. Unlike Alvaro, though, he worked methodically through the newspaper section by section, neatly refolding each section as he finished it and stacking the sections on the floor by his ottoman.

Kassy lounged on the big, overstuffed couch. The brightly colored, glossy ad pages were scattered around her, but she was poring over the Arts and Entertainment section. She frowned slightly, her lips moving as if she were silently rehearsing a speech, and Becca guessed that she was getting ready to try to persuade their parents that she should be allowed to go to some movie or other with her friends.

"When did Mom and Dad let you start going to R-rated movies, Becca?" she demanded.

"Probably next week, when I turn 17," Becca responded tartly.

"Not when I was 12—that's for sure! And once I'm 17, I'll probably still have to show them the reviews and explain why I think it's a movie worth seeing. Right, Dad?"

Mr. McKinnon looked at Becca over the top of his reading glasses and put down his section of newspaper. Kassy flashed Becca a look that Becca knew meant, "Uh-oh—Dad's going into lecture mode."

"Yes, I think we will still expect you to think through your choices and explain them to us," he said. "Discernment is always important, and the media is a good place to practice it because—"

"We know, Dad," Kassy interrupted. "We've already heard this speech about a jillion times before: 'Don't follow the crowd, don't be mindless, find out about a movie before you go see it.'" She rolled her eyes. "*Nobody* else has to research reviews before they go to a simple *movie*."

"Then I guess you have the distinction of being the best informed," Mr. McKinnon said mildly. "I'm proud to know that you're in a position to help your friends make good choices."

Kassy gave an exaggerated sigh and turned back to the movie review page. Mr. McKinnon winked conspiratorially at Becca before burying himself in the editorials again.

What would Dad say if he knew the choices I've been making? Becca thought unhappily. She shuffled into the kitchen to see if her mom was there.

Sure enough, Mrs. McKinnon sat at the big kitchen table, a half-empty mug of coffee beside her and manila folders and yellow legal pads spread in front of her.

"There's got to be a way," she muttered to herself. She ran her hand through her already disheveled brown hair.

"Whatcha working on, Mom?" Becca asked.

Mrs. McKinnon looked up. "Oh, Becca. I didn't hear you come in." She gestured to the mess of papers on the table. "I'm putting together an appeal to the zoning board's decision not to let us expand the homeless shelter. The board *says* they're worried about property values, but that's bunk. The shelter isn't in a high-priced area, and practically all the neighbors use the community center anyway. We've circulated a petition in the neighborhood—" Abruptly, Mrs. McKinnon stopped. "So—that's what's on my mind. What's on yours?"

"Well," Becca said, "I wondered if we could go for a walk."

Once Becca and her mom were on the trail in the undeveloped property behind their backyard, Becca found it was even harder to get started than she'd feared. Usually conversation flowed easily when she and her mom were in these woods, but not today. *Is this what happens when I keep things from my mom?* Becca wondered. *Pretty soon is it going to be too hard to tell her anything?*

"It's weird how many different kinds of things can happen in the woods," she said finally, thinking of the Wiccan circle, and her time alone with God afterward, and how this little piece of woodland stood for so much that was good in her relationship with her mom.

"Oh?" said her mother sharply, and she looked at Becca in a way that Becca didn't understand. "Is that what you want to tell me about?"

"Yeah," Becca nodded. "It's just . . . I'm not sure how to start."

"Is it about Nate?" her mother asked gently.

"Nate?" Becca said in complete bewilderment. "Why should it be about Nate?"

"Well," her mother said, "I know what can happen between couples in the woods. Your father and I were young once too, you know."

"*Mother!* Yuck! I don't want to hear about it!"

"I'm not saying we did anything we shouldn't have," Becca's mom explained. "I'm just saying I understand the temptation."

"Too much information," Becca said firmly. "I do *not* want to think about you and Dad like that. Anyway," she added, "you don't have to worry about me and Nate. We're not fooling around in the woods." She looked at her mom. "Is that what you think of us?"

Her mom thought for a moment. "No, I really don't. I think you and Nate have a healthy relationship. You respect each other." She paused. "But I know you've been upset about something. You haven't been yourself for, oh, a couple of weeks or more."

"Oh, Mom," Becca said, watching her feet on the trail so she wouldn't have to meet her mother's eyes, "I'm so sorry. I've been lying to you and Dad." Haltingly, she started to tell her mother the whole story, slowly at first, but then talking faster and faster because it was such a relief to get it out in the open.

"Well," was all her mother said when Becca finished. Becca shot a sideways glance at her. She thought her mom looked a little shell-shocked.

"Are you terribly disappointed in me?" she asked, gathering courage to look her mother in the eye.

Her mom didn't answer right away. "I am disappointed," she finally admitted slowly. "I like to think that we have the kind of relationship where you can tell us anything." She made a face. "I guess that's naïve."

Becca hung her head, but her mother put a finger under her chin and gently raised it. "But I'm proud of you for telling me now. That took courage. And I'm very glad that you came to the right decision about Wicca." She shook her head. "I guess you're old enough that you have to make some of those decisions on your own. It's hard for me to realize that your dad and I can't walk you through them all."

"Do you think we have to tell Dad?" Becca asked, biting her lip.

"Oh, yes," said her mom. "And I think you know that your father and I are going to want to hold you accountable about where you're going and what you're doing. It's not a punishment, Becca, but you're too precious for us to take risks with." She folded Becca into her arms and held her close. Becca snuggled against her mom and finally felt the tension draining out of her. It had been even harder than she'd thought to tell her mom, but she felt at last as if she was ready for a fresh start.

"Now," said her mother, giving Becca one final squeeze, "I think we'd better go back to the house and have a family conference."

• • •

"How could you have been so stupid?" Kassy screamed.

Becca was dumbfounded.

Earlier her parents had insisted that she tell Kassy what she had learned about Wicca. "For your own sake," her mother had said, "you have to put an end to *all* the secrecy. And for Kassy's sake," she continued, "you owe it to her to tell her the truth. She's looking to you more and more to see what it means to be growing up. If she finds out you've been exploring Wicca, who knows what she might think that gives her license to do. She needs to hear from you directly that you were wrong."

Well, clearly Kassy thought Becca was wrong. Becca looked out the window to make sure Alvaro wasn't hearing Kassy's screaming. Her parents had agreed that he was too young for this family conference and had sent him to play in the backyard with his favorite stick horse. He was galloping happily around the perimeter of the yard, waving his kid-sized cowboy hat wildly in the air.

Inside the kitchen, Kassy was waving her hands wildly in the air. "What were you thinking?" she shouted at Becca.

"I didn't know what I was doing at first," Becca stammered. "I mean, it all sounded so good. I thought it was a Christian group."

"Doing spells?" Kassy's voice rose to a shriek and cracked.

"Shhh. Calm down, Kassy." Mr. McKinnon got up from his chair and placed his hands on Kassy's shoulders. Gently he rubbed her shoulders, while at the same time settling her back into her chair. "Becca was deceived, and she made some bad decisions, but the point is that she realized she was wrong. That's not stupid."

"But she messed with *witches*," Kassy sobbed, tears starting to flow. "What if they're mad and start stalking her?"

"Oh, Kassy!" Suddenly Becca realized that Kassy wasn't angry at her; she was frightened for her. "Don't worry! I'll be okay."

"How can you be sure?" Kassy wailed. "I bet they have all kinds of spells and stuff you don't even know about."

"Kassy," Mr. McKinnon said firmly, "you do not ever have to live in fear about spells."

"Why?" sniffed Kassy. "Don't you believe they're real?"

"I have no idea," said Mr. McKinnon frankly. "I don't know if these Wiccans that Becca knows are calling on some real spiritual forces or just chanting nonsense or maybe a little of both. But what I *do* know is that the power of God is stronger than any power these so-called witches have. As Christians we have a greater power on our side than Wiccans ever will. Do you believe that?"

"Maybe," Kassy said uncertainly. "I mean, yeah, I believe it most of the time. For other people, anyway. But this is about Becca. Couldn't we call the police, just to be sure?"

Becca smiled at her sister. "Actually, one of the things I learned about Wicca from Katie is that it's a legal religion. I don't know what you could ask the police to do." She reached across the table to squeeze Kassy's hand. "I'll tell you something else I learned."

"What?" Kassy wiped her eyes.

"I learned that Dad was right about something."

"Oh, yeah?" Kassy said suspiciously.

"Remember when we did newspaper prayer a couple weeks ago and Dad said prayer has power?" Becca asked.

"No," Kassy said.

"Well, I remember," Becca persisted, "because I thought it was kind of a dumb cliché." She looked apologetically at her dad. "No offense."

"None taken," said her dad.

"Anyway," Becca continued awkwardly, "I've learned he was right. At least, I'm finding out that talking to God makes a difference to me." She felt self-conscious talking to Kassy like this, but she decided to keep going. "So if you want to do something to help me, Kass, I guess you could pray."

Kassy looked steadily at Becca, and Becca wondered what she was thinking. *Is she checking to see if I really mean it? Is she turned off because I sound too preachy?*

"Well, duh," Kassy finally said. "Of course I pray for you. The power of prayer isn't exactly a new idea, you know." She shook her head. "Sometimes you sure are slow to catch on."

chapter 19

"What was that all about on Saturday night?"

Becca gave her combination one last spin and opened the lock before looking up at Katie's accusing face.

"You mean my leaving your circle that way," she said, making it a statement, not a question.

"Exactly," Katie replied, leaning against the bank of school lockers. "I really took some heat for bringing you. You weakened the power when you broke the circle, you know," she said, lowering her voice.

"I don't care," Becca replied.

Katie's eyes widened. "It was obvious you were upset, but I thought by now you would have thought it over so that next time—"

"There won't be a next time," Becca said clearly. "I don't want anything more to do with Wicca."

"What do you mean?" Katie demanded. "I didn't bring you into the circle just to sightsee. I thought you were a sincere seeker."

"I was," Becca said. "And I learned what I needed to know about Wicca—that I'm not interested!"

Katie looked shocked. "How could you not be interested? We stand for everything important—power, the earth, kindness, doing good—"

"I thought you had some secret to spiritual power, but then I realized the only power I want is the power Jesus has."

Katie rolled her eyes. "That's such a narrow-minded answer," she said. "I told you, you can keep your Jesus and still do Wicca."

"No," said Becca firmly, "I can't." She had expected to feel nervous about facing Katie, but she felt surprisingly calm. *Kassy prayed about this at breakfast this morning*, she remembered. *I'll have to tell her thanks.*

"Your loss." Katie shrugged. "Listen, I'm going to have to ask you to keep silent about my circle. People might get the wrong idea."

"Trust me, I'm not going to do any advertising for you," Becca said. "But Katie, you need to know that I'm done with the secrecy thing. Don't worry—I'm not going to go around spreading rumors," she said as Katie began to protest. "But I'm not going to lie to anybody if they ask me about it."

Katie shrugged. "If that's the way it has to be, okay. But I think you're missing out." She gave Becca a pitying look and walked away.

• • •

"Thanks for letting me drop in on such short notice," Becca said as she let herself into Michelle Roberts' office at church.

"No problem. I usually try to keep my calendar open right after school in case anybody wants to come by to talk." She smiled and motioned for Becca to sit down. "So what's up?"

"I want to talk to you about that student leadership thing you told me about when we went to Copperchino's a while back."

Michelle leaned forward, elbows propped on her desk. Her eyes widened as if in anticipation. "Have you decided to give it a shot?"

"I'd like to," Becca said, "but I have to tell you something first." She paused. "Something you need to know before you decide if I'm qualified to be a student leader."

"Go ahead," Michelle said and smiled. "I'm listening."

Becca told Michelle about how she'd walked blindly into Wicca, thinking it was something else. She admitted that she kept exploring it even after she found out what it was because by then, she had questions about whether Christianity really *was* the only way. She described how she deceived her parents and resisted Jacie's and Tyler's attempts to talk to her about it. Finally she told Michelle about how she'd realized that she truly *did* want Jesus alone to be the center of her life.

"When you first asked me about being a student leader, I wasn't sure I wanted to do it," she concluded. "Now I want to, but I'm not sure I'm the kind of role model you're looking for."

"We've established some very specific requirements for our student leaders," Michelle said. "I told you about them before; do you remember?"

"Sure," Becca said. She'd gone over and over them in her mind before she decided to approach Michelle.

"Tell me," Michelle prompted.

"First, you have to be a committed Christian and be willing and able to say so. Second, be active and faithful in church and youth group. Third, be willing to report to the youth board and accept their supervision and guidance."

"Right!" Michelle gave a brisk little nod. "Now answer your own question. Do you measure up to those three things?"

"I do *now*," Becca said, "but I didn't always. I wasn't very committed or faithful or willing to be accountable a few weeks ago."

"So," Michelle said, a smile twitching the corners of her mouth, "you know firsthand how God can change a life. That's a good thing. You know, Becca," she added seriously, "*everyone* goes through times of doubt—even leaders. It's what you do with your doubts that's important."

"I'm still kind of confused about that," Becca said. "I know you can't have both Wicca and Jesus, but how is it that so much of Wicca sounds like Christianity? That's the kind of doubt that got me wondering if Wicca was okay in the first place."

"Give me some examples," Michelle said.

"Well, Katie talks about praying, for instance," Becca said. "And devotions, and angels. She even did that thing of writing sins on paper and burning them, like we did once on a retreat. Was that a Wiccan spell when we did it on retreat?"

"It most certainly was not," Michelle said. "It was a concrete example of how God's forgiveness wipes out our sin."

"See—that's what I don't get," Becca said. "How can we be doing the same things as Wicca? Is that part of Wicca good? Or is it good when we do it and bad when they do it?"

Michelle nodded. "Those are really good questions. Do you know that the easiest way to deceive somebody is by taking the truth and giving it a gentle twist?"

Becca thought a moment. "Like saying I'm going out with the group and letting my mom think I meant the youth group when really I meant the Wicca group."

"Right," Michelle said. "That's what happens with a lot of good, true, biblical things—like prayer, for instance. You think 'prayer' always means God-honoring, God-centered prayer, so you're caught off guard when people twist prayer into something different."

"That's what got me mixed up in this whole thing to start with," Becca said. "When Katie started talking about prayer, I figured she meant, you know, talking-to-God prayer." Becca thought about this a little. "I can tell the difference between Christian prayer and Wicca prayer now, but I can't really define it."

"Want me to give it a go?" Michelle asked.

Becca nodded.

"Okay," Michelle said. "Here are three standards you can use to determine if a prayer is a God-focused prayer. First, you have to pray to the God of the Bible, not just some 'spirit' or 'supreme being.' Make sense?"

"Uh-huh," Becca said. "Katie talked about 'the lord,' but later I realized she didn't mean the Lord I know from the Bible."

"So that's one guideline for when you pray," Michelle said. "Here's another: The Bible tells us to pray honestly and humbly. We should ask God for what we need, but we shouldn't try to manipulate Him."

"Wow!" Becca said. She felt like a cartoon character when the lightbulb goes on over his head. "Manipulating—that's exactly what Wicca prayer is about. Not in an underhanded, sneaky kind of way—I don't mean that. But Katie talked as if she could control the outcome of her prayer by doing the right steps—lighting a candle and saying the right words and stuff."

"Exactly." Michelle beamed at Becca. "But you don't manipulate God. He's in control and decides the final outcome, not you."

Becca sat quietly for a moment or two, just soaking this idea in. "I think that's what attracted me to Wicca, though," she admitted softly. "The idea that I could be in control and make things come out the way I wanted them to."

"Well, get over it," Michelle said bluntly. "You're not in charge. And no offense, but you'd probably do a pretty lousy job if you were." She grinned and the laugh lines in her face deepened. "And I mean that in the most loving way possible."

Becca groaned. "You are so right."

"Okay. Final prayer tip: Pray in Jesus' name. Simple, huh?" Michelle said.

Becca smacked herself on the forehead. "If I'd remembered that, I would never have gotten suckered by Wicca," she said. "Now that I think about it, I never heard the name of Jesus except when I asked Katie about it." She made a face. "Kassy was right."

"Right about what?" Michelle asked.

"I was really stupid."

Michelle raised her eyebrows. "I wouldn't say you were stupid. Wicca is a very fast-growing religion. That doesn't make it right, but it does mean you're not the only one who's fallen for it. Like you found out, there's a lot about it that's pretty attractive on the surface. And parts of it sound similar to Christianity—just like with any other religion that seems to have the same concepts and beliefs as Christianity. It's important to always dig deeper. That's when you find the problems and differences. You have to learn to ask the right questions, that's all."

Becca shook her head doubtfully. "But how do you know which are the right questions and which are the wrong questions? I mean, once I knew it was Wicca, I started wondering whether the church was telling the truth about Wicca. You wouldn't say that was a good thing."

"Sure I would! Becca, I'm never afraid that the truth won't stand up to some hard questions. And remember," Michelle said, the smile disappearing from her face, "the Christian church has had its share of false leaders. We need to be discerning about everything—and that includes what you hear in church."

"You've been talking to my dad," Becca accused. "That's his theme song: discernment."

"Your dad's a smart man," Michelle said.

"Yeah, I guess," Becca agreed. "So are you saying that all questions are good questions?"

Michelle thought for a moment. "I suppose you could come up with an extreme example that would be an exception—but, generally, yes, I would say that questions are good. The thing is, some questions can lead you into dangerous places if you're asking them on your own. Do you know what I mean?"

"I think so," Becca said slowly. "You mean if I hadn't kept my questions about Wicca a secret, somebody could have helped me see through it sooner." She made a face. "But you don't always want to tell your mom and dad everything! Or your youth leader," she added apologetically.

Michelle just smiled. Becca had the feeling she was waiting for Becca to figure something out.

"Oh!" Becca exclaimed suddenly. "Jacie! Jacie and Tyler! They were asking me the right questions and sharing their concerns, but

I didn't want to hear them." She smacked her forehead again. "I *was* stupid!"

Michelle laughed and just shook her head.

Becca stood up and walked to the window and fiddled with the cord on the miniblind. "Michelle, do you really mean it when you say it's okay to ask questions about anything?"

"Yes," Michelle answered.

"I'm still kind of curious about the spells. Do they do anything, or not?"

"I honestly don't know, Becca," Michelle said, sitting down again. "I do know that there are spiritual forces we can't see. The Bible tells us that. Whether Wicca taps into those forces or not, I'm not qualified to judge."

"Are you talking about devil worship?" Becca asked. "Because I asked—Katie's not into anything like that."

"No," agreed Michelle. "As far as I know, people who practice Wicca aren't devil worshipers. But that doesn't mean that Satan can't use Wicca without Wiccans being aware of it."

"Like asking the goddess into themselves," Becca said. "That's what really scared me. I didn't know if there was something that might really come in."

"And you were wise not to find out," Michelle said. "But on the other hand, a lot of spells sound to me more like wishful thinking or just good psychology than anything else." She swiveled in her chair and pulled a book off the bookshelf behind her.

"What's that?" Becca asked. She noticed that the book had been on the shelf the wrong way, so she couldn't read its title.

"A book on witchcraft for teens," Michelle said. "I keep the spine turned to the back of the shelf so the church board members don't wander in and get the wrong idea."

"I think *I* might be getting the wrong idea," Becca said. "Why are you reading about spells?"

"So I can answer questions like yours, of course," Michelle said. "What—did you think youth ministry is all Bible studies and laser tag?" She flipped through the book. "Okay, here's what I mean. I'm going to show you this because I know you've already seen some of this stuff in action, and because I trust you not to try it out." She looked Becca in the eye. "Right?"

"Right!" said Becca fervently.

"Even if it sounds silly, it's not something to play with," Michelle warned. "Because we don't know when spiritual forces opposed to God might be involved. That said, check out this 'spell' for helping you to resist drugs. Take away all the candles and circles and what do you have?"

Becca studied the page carefully. "Pretty much it's just repeating to yourself to be strong and use self-control," she said.

"Yup," agreed Michelle. "So suppose your friend Katie repeats this little chant to herself before she goes to a party, and says it again when somebody offers her one of those designer pills. If she says no, is it because the spell worked? Or because she was reminding herself not to give in?"

"I don't know." Becca shook her head. "Which is it?"

"I don't know either," said Michelle. "I'm not convinced that this so-called spell is any more than a good pep talk. But that doesn't mean all spells are so innocent. In fact, I wouldn't say *any* spells are innocent, whether they 'work' or not." She flipped open the Bible on her desk and thumbed through the pages until she found the passage she wanted. "Listen. This is Deuteronomy 18, verses 10 through 12. 'There shall not be found among you . . . one who practices witchcraft . . . or one who casts a spell . . . For whoever does these things is detestable to the Lord.' "

"So . . . does that mean it's real, or not?" Becca asked.

"Let me ask you a different question," Michelle said. "Is it God's way or not?"

"Not!" Becca said without hesitation.

"One more question," Michelle said, leaning forward and speaking with quiet intensity. "Is Jesus real?"

"Totally," Becca said. And she gave Michelle a quick, strong nod of her own.

chapter 20

"Hi, Angela!" Becca called to the receptionist in the Outreach Community Center lobby. "I'm supposed to pick up my mom. Do you know if her meeting is over yet?"

"Sure is, Honey," Angela answered. "And I'll tell you what—that city zoning board is gonna be sorry they ever tangled with your mama! Do you know that in that meeting she sweet-talked D. G. Hart into working on an appeal for free? Why, he's one of the biggest lawyers in town!"

"I've heard of him," Becca said. "His wife's a writer, isn't she?"

"Could be," Angela agreed. "She'll have some story to write about before this thing's over, that's sure." She shook her head. "Your mama's going to keep worrying that zoning board till they *beg* her to build on to the center."

"I hope so!" Becca said. "Where's my mom now?"

"In the staff room—sitting with her feet up, I do hope," Angela said. "She deserves a rest. Oh, and Becca—" she called as Becca turned to go. "There's a message here for you."

"For me?" Becca said. "Who from?"

"Well, now, I don't remember just offhand," Angela said, sifting through a stack of memos and notes. "Call came in today just when the after-school program buses were dropping off and things were a little busy. That's why it almost slipped my mind just now. But I wrote it down for you." She pulled a page from a pink message pad and handed it to Becca. "Here it is."

Becca looked at the note, then her eyes got wide. "Angela!" she shrieked, lunging across the receptionist's counter to throw her arms around the older woman's neck. "It's from Otis!"

"Well, now, isn't that nice," Angela said, patting Becca's shoulder. "I'm glad it's good news, Honey." Gently, she disengaged Becca. "You're pretty excited about this Otis. What about that nice Nate who comes here sometimes to help out with the rec program? I thought it was him you were sweet on."

"Oh, I *am*," Becca assured her. "I mean, maybe 'sweet on him' isn't exactly how I would describe it . . ." She blushed under Angela's knowing smile. "But, yeah—Nate's the one. Otis is just a friend of mine. He got hurt last month and I never heard what happened to him. I can't believe he called here!" Eagerly, she read aloud the rest of the message. "Otis called. Said to tell Becca he's okay, keep praying, he met a friend of hers, and he'll be back in the harness when he gets the casts off and out of rehab."

"Oh, I remember that call now," Angela said. "Back in the harness—that's a funny thing to say. Is he a farmer of some kind?"

"No," Becca laughed. "He's a paraglider. Where was he calling from, Angela? You didn't write his number down."

"Well, come to think of it, he didn't give me a number."

"Oh, no!" Becca wailed. "How can I call him back?"

"I don't know, Honey," Angela said. "I'm sorry. I guess I just thought if he was a friend of yours, you'd know how to reach him. He knew how to find you, after all."

Becca pressed her lips together hard to keep from crying out her disappointment. It wasn't Angela's fault, after all. She couldn't know how hard and how unsuccessfully Becca had tried to track Otis. "I don't even know his last name," she explained to Angela. "And he doesn't know mine. He just knows that I volunteer here—that's why he called here instead of my house."

Angela shook her head slowly. "Well, that's a real shame. If I'd have known, I'd have surely gotten his number for you." Her face brightened, and she pointed to the note in Becca's hand. "But he says he met a friend of yours. Maybe your friend will tell you where Otis is." She looked inquiringly at Becca.

"He must have made a mistake," Becca said, frustrated. She stared at the message as if somehow it might tell her something more if only she read it enough times. "Since everyone knows I've been worrying about Otis," she said finally, "I'm sure if someone met him they would have told me about it." She shrugged. Then she smiled and nodded. "I bet he's talking about one of the other paragliders. I'll ask around next time I go gliding."

"And if he calls again, I'll be sure to get a number for you," Angela promised.

Becca's eyes lit up. "That's right! He could call again! I hadn't thought of that. Thanks, Angela!" She carefully folded the message and tucked it in her pocket. *I'll put it on my bulletin board when I get home*, she decided. *I'm sure that one way or another I'll hear from Otis again.*

• • •

Conversation over supper that night was an excited babble of updates on Mrs. McKinnon's meeting with the attorney and conjectures about where Otis might be.

"The message says 'when he gets the *casts* off,' " Kassy pointed out, examining the note before handing it back to Becca. "Not just one cast, but lots."

"Or at least two," Mr. McKinnon pointed out reasonably.

"At *least* two," Kassy said with emphasis. "*And* he's in rehab. So he's still in a hospital somewhere. He must have gotten hurt really bad."

"Maybe that's why he didn't get in touch with you sooner," Mrs. McKinnon suggested to Becca. "I wonder what prompted him to call now."

"He said he wanted me to keep praying," Becca said slowly. "But that's weird."

"What's so weird about that?" Kassy demanded.

"Nothing, except Otis always blew me off when I talked about God."

"Sometimes non-Christians are glad to have people praying for them, though," Mrs. McKinnon said thoughtfully.

"I suppose," Becca agreed, not fully convinced.

"Maybe he's feeling the need for prayer more now that's he's hurt," her dad suggested. "I'm proud that he thinks of you as someone he can ask to pray," he added with a smile.

"I can pray for Otis too," Kassy said quickly. "It's not like Becca's the only one in the family who prays."

"Pray, family! Pray!" Alvaro chimed in. The rest of the family turned to look at him, and he beamed, apparently delighted with the attention. "God bless!" he shouted, clapping his hands. "Amen!"

● ● ●

When Becca was finished loading the dishwasher after supper, she went to her dad's office. Her dad was at the computer, so she stood quietly in the doorway so as not to disturb him.

"Are you working on something important, Dad?" she asked after a minute or two.

"Becca! I didn't know you were there," he said. "Come in. I'm not working at all." He grinned sheepishly. "I came in to check e-mail and got distracted by a game of Elf Bowling."

Becca picked a stack of books off a chair and set them on the floor. She sat down and tucked her feet under her. She knew what she wanted to talk about, but she wasn't quite sure how to begin. "You know how we were talking about prayer tonight at supper," she finally said, picking at a loose thread in the chair's upholstery.

"Uh-huh," her dad murmured encouragingly.

"Well, what I'm wondering is, why doesn't prayer always work?" Becca shot a glance at her dad to see his reaction, then turned her attention back to the thread.

"I don't know," her dad said thoughtfully.

Becca turned to stare at her dad. "You don't know? You're supposed to have the answer!"

"Sorry, but that's not a department I'm in charge of," her dad said. "I can help you ask some more good questions, though. For instance, what do you mean when you say *prayer doesn't work?*"

"That I—" Becca began, then stopped short. "Well, I guess I mean that I don't get what I ask for."

Her dad nodded. "That's what I usually mean, too," he agreed.

"So . . . maybe sometimes I'm asking for the wrong thing?" Becca asked.

"Are you?"

Becca bit her lip. "I remember praying that we wouldn't adopt Alvaro," she admitted. "I'm glad God didn't give me what I wanted that time. But sometimes I know what I'm asking for is a good thing," she persisted. "Like when I asked God to show me whether Wicca was right or not. I remember standing in the hall, talking to Katie and Solana, and asking God to let me know whether I should go to the circle or not. And He didn't answer."

"No?"

"No. I remember I was trying to decide fast because Hannah was coming and I didn't want her to hear . . ." Becca trailed to a stop. "You don't mean that *Hannah* could have been the way God answered that prayer, do you?"

"What do you think?"

"It could have been a coincidence that she came along just then," Becca said.

"If you believe in coincidence," her dad agreed.

"Okay, let me give you another example," Becca said quickly. "I've been praying for Solana to become a Christian. I've got to believe God wants that, too. So why hasn't she become a Christian?"

"Yet," her dad added.

"What do you mean?"

"Solana hasn't become a Christian *yet*," he said.

"Do you mean that Solana *is* going to become a Christian some day?" Becca asked.

"I don't know," her dad said. "That's another area that's not my department. But I do know that it's too soon to say God won't answer that prayer." He swiveled his chair to face Becca directly. "I have lots of examples of seemingly unanswered prayer in my life, too," he said. "And I can't always explain them. But I also know—absolutely know—that sometimes God answers my prayers in real and clear ways. Have you ever experienced that?"

Becca put her hand in her pocket and fingered the message from Otis. She thought of all the times she prayed that he would be okay. Then she thought about talking with God in the woods the night she broke away from the circle. Nothing could make her doubt the real presence of God in that time of prayer. "Yeah," she answered. "Yeah, I've experienced that."

● ● ●

"Do you think anybody will come?" Jacie asked, fidgeting in the desk chair and watching the classroom door.

"What do you mean?" Tyler said. "We're here, aren't we?"

"I mean anybody *else*—we don't count," Jacie said. "What if nobody else comes?"

"They'll come," Hannah said. "We've been praying about it."

"And we put up all those signs," Nate added. "After all the fuss the school paper made about whether it was legal to advertise a Bible study on campus, I don't think there's anybody who *doesn't* know about today's meeting."

"That's almost worse," Jacie said. "Oh, Becca, aren't you nervous about starting this group?"

"No," said Becca, her eyes shining. "I'm pumped."

"But you said anybody could come and ask any questions they want," Jacie said. "I would never know what to say."

"If I don't know, I'll just say so and then I'll go look it up," Becca said. "It's okay not to have all the answers. It's not like I have to be in control." She gave a small smile. *Thanks for that tip, Michelle*, she thought.

"I guess Solana isn't coming," Hannah said. "Not that I expected her to, but I hoped . . ." She broke off as students started coming into the classroom and finding places to sit in the desks that Becca had pulled into a semicircle. Becca and her friends spent the next several minutes with introductions.

"Well," Becca said when everyone was settled and the classroom door closed to limit distractions, "I guess we can start. Thanks for coming. The idea for this group is to have a place where anyone can ask honest questions about what the Bible says about who we are and who God is—whether you believe in Jesus or not."

"Not," said a guy who had introduced himself as Mike. "Just so you know."

Becca grinned. "And just so *you* know right up front," she said, "I *am* a follower of Jesus."

The door opened and she looked up.

"Sorry I'm late," panted Solana. "I brought a friend." Following hesitantly behind her was Kara from the Wicca circle. "I'm Solana, and this is Kara," Solana said to the group, "and we have lots of questions."

Solana's eyes met Becca's over the heads of the other students, and she smiled at Becca. "I'm not signing up for anything, but I'm ready to listen to some answers."

FOCUS ON THE FAMILY®

Welcome to the Family!

Whether you received this book as a gift, borrowed it, or purchased it yourself, we're glad you read it. It's just one of the many helpful, insightful, and encouraging resources produced by Focus on the Family.

In fact, that's what Focus on the Family is all about — providing inspiration, information, and biblically based advice to people in all stages of life.

It began in 1977 with the vision of one man, Dr. James Dobson, a licensed psychologist and author of 18 best-selling books on marriage, parenting, and family. Alarmed by the societal, political, and economic pressures that were threatening the existence of the American family, Dr. Dobson founded Focus on the Family with one employee and a once-a-week radio broadcast aired on only 36 stations.

Now an international organization, the ministry is dedicated to preserving Judeo-Christian values and strengthening and encouraging families through the life-changing message of Jesus Christ. Focus ministries reach families worldwide through 10 separate radio broadcasts, two television news features, 13 publications, 18 Web sites, and a steady series of books and award-winning films and videos for people of all ages and interests.

• • •

For more information about the ministry, or if we can be of help to your family, simply write to Focus on the Family, Colorado Springs, CO 80995 or call (800) A-FAMILY (232-6459). Friends in Canada may write Focus on the Family, PO Box 9800, Stn Terminal, Vancouver, BC V6B 4G3 or call (800) 661-9800. Visit our Web site — www.family.org — to learn more about Focus on the Family or to find out if there is an associate office in your country.

We'd love to hear from you!

love

Want More? Life
Go from ordinary to extraordinary! *Want More? Life* will help you open the door to God's abundant life. You'll go deeper, wider and higher in your walk with God in the midst of everyday challenges like self-image, guys, friendships and big decisions. Spiral hardcover.

Want More? Love
You may ask, "Does God really love me? How can He love me — with all my faults and flaws?" *Want More? Love* is a powerful devotional that shows you how passionately and protectively God loves and cares for you — and how you can love Him in return! Spiral hardcover.

Bloom: A Girl's Guide to Growing Up

You have lots of questions about life. In *Bloom: A Girl's Guide To Growing Up*, your questions are addressed and answered with the honesty youth expect and demand. From changing bodies, to dating and sex, to relationships, money and more, girls will find the answers they need. Paperback.

Brio

It's the inside scoop — with hot tips on everything from fashion and fitness to real-life faith. Monthly magazine.

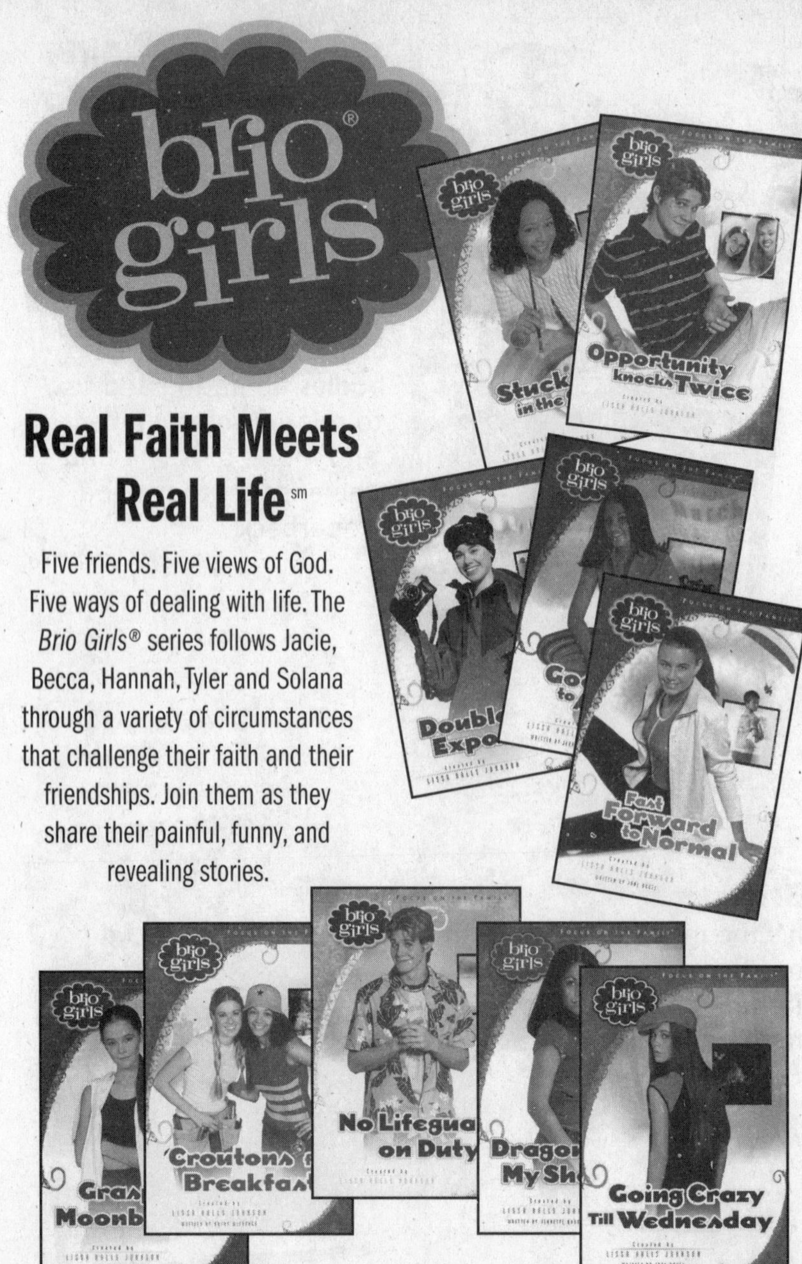
brio girls®
Real Faith Meets Real Life℠
Five friends. Five views of God. Five ways of dealing with life. The *Brio Girls®* series follows Jacie, Becca, Hannah, Tyler and Solana through a variety of circumstances that challenge their faith and their friendships. Join them as they share their painful, funny, and revealing stories.
Opportunity Knocks Twice
Fast Forward to Normal
Going Crazy Till Wednesday